The Seventeen Steps Adventure

The Seventeen Steps Adventure
by
Chris Wright

© Chris Wright 2017

ISBN: 978-1-5203448-6-7

Also available as an e-Book ISBN: 978-0-9954549-6-5

Website: www.whitetreepublishing.com
More books by Chris Wright on
www.rocky-island.com
Email: wtpbristol@gmail.com

The Seventeen Steps Adventure is a work of fiction. Names, characters, places, and incidents are the product of the author's imagination or are used fictitiously.

The Bible verses in this story are taken from *"The Holy Bible, English Standard Version. ESV® Permanent Text Edition® (2016). Copyright © 2001 by Crossway Bibles, a publishing ministry of Good News Publishers."*

(See also www.youversion.com for free downloads of over a thousand Bible translations in over a thousand languages on your phone, tablet, and computer.)

Published by
White Tree Publishing
Bristol
UNITED KINGDOM

A Word from the Author

I first wrote this story some time ago, and things have now changed a lot, especially with electronics and digital communication. No mobile (cell) phones, digital cameras, tablets and computers back then. So although the main story is unchanged, some things have been updated to make the adventure happen today.

Cameras changed from film to digital for everyday use in just a few short years. Most phones now have excellent cameras in them, and of course the results can be seen immediately. So for Ryan in this story, who has only ever seen digital cameras, the idea of trying out his Gran's old-fashioned camera using *film* is fun. And to hear that the film has to be processed before he can see if the pictures are successful, comes as a big shock!

A few things to note. In America a mother is a mom, while over on Ryan's side of the Atlantic a mother is a mum. Fathers are usually known as dad on both sides. Trainers in England are what are known as sneakers in America, and Americans call the English pavement the sidewalk. Holidays are vacations, and there are other differences, especially in the way some words are spelt. This book uses the British English spelling because that's where the adventure takes place.

Measurements

The measurements in this book are in miles, feet and inches. Here is an approximate table of conversion to metric.

1 mile is 1.6km

1 yard is a little less than 1m

1 foot is 30cm

1 inch is 2.5cm

I hope this helps!

Chapters

Chapter One

Ryan stopped running and stared in surprise. A camera lay on the park bench, and there was no one sitting with it. He looked around. The park seemed empty. He could tell it was a good model.

"Wow!" he said to himself almost silently, afraid of being overheard. "Someone's left it. Forgotten all about it I expect."

Ryan turned quickly as he heard footsteps on the path. A woman with a dog was coming. Perhaps the camera was hers. No, she walked straight past, the dog pulling on its lead as though in a hurry to get home.

Ryan was also in a hurry now. In a hurry to get home with the camera. He'd wanted a camera of his own for a long time. Of course, he'd never imagined he would get one as expensive as this. Carefully he picked it up and examined it. The camera definitely looked expensive. Very expensive indeed.

Ryan started to run. He was good at running, and his teacher said he was the fastest runner they'd had in his year for a long time.

As he left the park, he stopped to look at the camera again. He studied the large screen on the back and wondered if he dared switch the camera on. Only for a moment. Just to check it worked and hadn't been left on the park bench because it was no good.

He pressed the *on* switch and the lens in the front moved out. A picture of the street filled the screen. The camera seemed to be working. And then Ryan knew. He'd known all along really. The camera wasn't his to keep. It was only lost.

He could try to find the owner — or take it to the police station. If nobody called for it at the police station, he might be able to keep it. He remembered how a girl at school had found a watch once. She'd taken it to the police station, and ages later she'd been told she could keep it because no one had claimed it.

It might be the same with the camera. The person who'd lost it mightn't want it back. Ryan looked down at the shiny black casing. No, that was silly. *Anyone* would want a camera like this.

"What you got there?"

On the way into the park he'd taken no notice of four bikers riding two up on two off-road motorbikes waiting by the gates. He had to go past them now.

"Give it here, kid. It's too smart for you to carry round like that."

He stared at the rider on the front of the bike. His face was covered by a black visor. He sounded young. There were four riders. Two up on each bike. One looked like a girl.

The camera was theirs! No it wasn't. They'd not asked for it back. They were going to steal it!

He held it tightly and looked round for anyone who could help. Mr. Stanbury who lived in his road was walking his way.

Mr. Stanbury was a builder who looked tough. He stopped and looked at the riders. "Problem?" he asked Ryan.

The riders took one look at Mr. Stanbury, started their bikes and moved off, their engines sounding like a swarm of angry bees. "We'll be back," one of them called.

"It's okay," Ryan said to his rescuer, glad to see the bikes disappear down the road. "But thanks for coming at the right time. I found this camera in the park and they wanted it. It's not theirs. I don't know whose it is."

"Take it to the police station," Mr. Stanbury said. "That's the thing to do."

Ryan nodded. "Yes, that's what I thought."

Mr. Stanbury told Ryan to take care, and moved off.

The problem was, there wasn't a police station anywhere nearby that he could think of. Gran might know of one. His Gran lived in a turning off the long straight road opposite the park. Yes, Gran would know where to take it.

He found Gran doing the washing. She shut the door of the washing machine and switched it on. The machine started making a loud hissing sound as the water began to run in.

"We can't talk in here properly," she said to Ryan. "We'd better go into the garden."

Ryan found himself being led gently by the shoulder out into the small back garden that always looked so neat and tidy. "My, that's a smart camera you've got there."

Ryan felt proud of it for a moment. Then he remembered he was here for advice. "Gran, it's not mine. I found it in the park. I'm going to take it to the police station." He wasn't going to mention the bikes.

Gran took the camera carefully. "I'll come with you if you like. I have to go down to the shops. Unless...." The camera was upside-down now, in Gran's hands. She adjusted her glasses. "There's a sticker with a name here, and there's an address I think. You have a look, Ryan. You've got sharp eyes."

Ryan took the camera. He'd been afraid this would happen. The last thing he wanted was for the camera to go back to its owner. "Yes, Gran, it's a name and address. E. Harrington. Six Bellevue Terrace. That's not far."

Gran smiled. "Then I'm sure E. Harrington, whoever that is, will be glad to get it back. An expensive camera, I should think. Perhaps there'll be a reward."

"A reward? A *reward?*" Yes, Ryan decided, there was sure to be a reward. Such a valuable camera as this would be bound to have a rich owner.

Ryan knew quite a bit about cameras. Not about each different model. But he knew which were expensive makes and which were just cheap, ordinary ones. There was a camera shop quite close to home where he sometimes looked in the window.

It would be a long time before he could afford an expensive camera like this. Not until he left school and had a job to go to. But with the reward he might be able to buy one of the cheaper models. They probably worked quite well, and certainly much better than the camera on his old phone. If he could afford a new camera, it wouldn't look as special as this one. This one was definitely special. It had nearly been his, but to keep it now would be stealing.

As he left the house he looked carefully in both directions. Surely those four bikers wouldn't be hanging around here. No sign of them. He switched the camera on and pointed it in the direction of Bellevue Terrace. Then, looking at the screen, he marched off to claim his reward.

Chapter Two

Ryan knew Bellevue Terrace was a smart road, with what must be expensive houses. The people who lived here were probably really, really rich. Ryan wondered just what sort of reward he would get. Money, almost certainly. He could imagine it to himself. Being shown into a large room and offered an envelope packed full of money.

He smiled. It probably wouldn't be like that at all. Even so, he ought to get quite a generous reward. Enough to buy *some* sort of camera for himself. It would have a zoom lens. It would have a really bright flash. It would, in fact, probably work almost as well as the one in his hands. Being honest and returning the camera was a good thing to do, he told himself. God would be pleased about that.

Ryan felt he didn't know very much about God yet. Gran did, and she took him to church. There was a young people's group there, and Ryan went every Sunday now. He was getting to like it, and some of his school friends went as well. Even though he knew only a little about God, he knew God wanted people to be honest. He was being honest now. So as long as God was watching, there was sure to be a fantastic reward.

Here it is, he thought to himself — Bellevue Terrace. The houses were large, and not all joined up in long rows like his own and Gran's. They had front gardens too, with a gate onto a drive with a garage. Ryan found number six and went up to the imposing, white front door. He rang the bell, pulled his zip jacket straight, and waited rather nervously for someone to answer.

A young man opened the door after a long wait. "Yes?" He looked down at Ryan and saw the camera. "Ah, you've found it. Not been using it, I hope."

Ryan held onto the camera tightly. "It says E. Harrington on the camera," he said. "Is it yours?"

"Sort of. Well, it's my father's actually, but he lets me use it." The young man tried to take it from Ryan. "Not damaged it, have you?"

Ryan held the camera up to show it was undamaged. He didn't like the man at all. "Is there — a reward?"

The man snatched the camera out of Ryan's hands, shook his head and closed the door. Not a word of thanks, and not a mention of any money. Ryan stayed on the doorstep in case the young man came back, but the white front door stayed firmly shut. So he went slowly out through the gate. It had been shut when he arrived, but Ryan kicked it back against the rockery stones. He felt fed up.

It wasn't much good being honest after all. He

hadn't even been thanked. As if he'd damaged it in any way! As if he would! He knew much more about being careful with delicate equipment than to do that. And what had God been doing all the time? Wasn't he supposed to be watching and caring for people?

Ryan didn't feel like going home just yet. He would go back to Gran and watch the telly until the midmorning news came on. Then, and only then, would he go home for lunch. On the way, he kept a careful eye open for the bikers. He had a feeling they were going to be trouble.

Chapter Three

He couldn't bring himself to tell his Gran what had happened at the house in Bellevue Terrace. She soon found out, though. Gran had a way of finding things out, without asking lots of nosey questions. She had a way of just understanding how you felt, without needing to say anything.

She put her arm around him as he sat hunched in the large armchair in her back room watching a programme about two people who wanted to find a house in the countryside. The programme was stupid, he decided. He shook Gran's arm free and reached for the remote to switch the set off.

"Why didn't I get a reward?" he asked, feeling extremely cross.

"Is that why you returned it?" Gran asked.

"Yes ... no ... not really. I took it back because you found the name and address on it. It wasn't mine, anyway."

Gran nodded wisely. "You took it back because it wasn't yours. It was mean of that young man not to give you something as a sort of thank you. If I'd been there I'd have given him a piece of my mind, I can tell you! "

Ryan started to laugh. "I wish you *had* been there, Gran. You'd have been ever so good." He became serious for a moment. "Why didn't God tell him off? God could have *made* him give me a reward. God can do anything."

"Yes, Ryan, so he can. But you mustn't expect a reward every time you do something good."

He nodded. "I know what you mean, Gran. All the same, I did so want a reward so I could buy one of my own. The camera on my mobile phone is rubbish. Could you buy me a camera, Gran, as a sort of birthday present in advance?"

Gran laughed. "You've not long had your last birthday! Your generation doesn't know they're born, Ryan. When your dad was young, he never would have dreamed anyone could have such a thing as a mobile phone, and certainly not one that took photographs you could see on the screen immediately. The film had to be developed before you could tell if the picture had come out."

"Developed?"

"There was a roll of film you had to take to the chemist or camera shop, hand it in, and wait a couple of days or maybe a week to get the prints back."

"Wow, almost prehistoric. How did people manage in those days?"

Gran laughed again. "I'll tell you what. If you really want to know how people managed in those days, I've got an old camera put away upstairs. If you like, I'll look it out for you later this evening, and you can see it if you come round in the morning. And bring your cousin Natalie. She arrives from America later today, don't forget."

His face filled with excitement and then disappointment. Was this something he wanted to share with his American cousin? "I don't want to wait until tomorrow. Could you look for it *now*!"

Gran smiled. "Just like your father was — impatient. All right, we'll go up and look for it. It's nothing very special, mind. Nothing like those fancy modern cameras. Just an old camera in a brown leather case. It works all right — at least it did last time it was used."

Ryan shrugged. Any camera would be interesting, even a prehistoric one that took film. He made his way up the steep stairs and watched while Gran opened the landing cupboard. There were clothes, boxes of books, some old gramophone records and even a huge family Bible. The Bible was falling apart at the back. There was no sign of the camera.

"I don't think it's going to be in here, Ryan. By the way, did I ever show you this Bible? It's too old to use now, but I still like to keep it for all the memories it's got inside. In the front the family have recorded the names of every baby born into the family for the past hundred and forty years.

Your name is entered in there and so is your father's. Lift it down and we can have a look at it."

The Bible was heavy, and Ryan carried it to the small chest at the top of the stairs. He watched while Gran opened the front few pages. There were all sorts of names neatly written, some in black ink and some in blue.

"My eyes aren't too good, but I think that's your father. Michael Edward it says."

Ryan knew his father's name was Michael, but not Edward as well. "Why Edward?" he asked.

"Your grandfather was called Edward. There, you can see his name. And there's *your* name! "

"Wow," Ryan said, "it's exciting, isn't it! If I get married and have children, they'll be put in there. Then one day they'll read their names for themselves. You must look after this old Bible carefully, Gran." He felt quite concerned.

"I shall, Ryan, I shall. I have a much newer one to use for myself, as you well know. This Bible has exactly the same things in, but the words can sometimes be difficult for young people to understand. Now then, we haven't found the old camera."

Ryan was still reading the neat handwriting. "Who's this, Gran? After my dad's name, it says John Kenneth. Who's John Kenneth?"

Ryan's Gran smiled. "That's your Uncle Jack."

"I know about Uncle Jack," Ryan said firmly.

"Dad's gone to meet him and his family at the airport. When did he change his name?"

"Jack is short for John, dear."

"It can't be *short* for John," Ryan protested. "It's just as long!"

"Perhaps it is." Gran sighed. "Perhaps it is. Anyway, it's supposed to be short for John, but you're right, of course."

There had been a lot of talk in the family about Uncle Jack. Uncle Jack had gone to America many years ago and got married soon afterwards. Now he was coming back for business up in London, and he'd have his wife and daughter with him. Ryan had seen them a few times online.

Their daughter was called Natalie, and she was the same age as him. It seemed funny to think there were people in his family he'd only ever seen on the internet. He wasn't sure if he wanted to meet his American cousin face to face. She mightn't be fun to be with, and the half term break from school might seem very long if he was stuck with her all week.

Gran reached into the space that had been hidden by the large Bible. She pulled out a brown leather case the size of a book. It was surely too big to hold a camera.

Ryan watched while Gran opened it and pulled out something flat covered in black leather with shiny chrome bits. A very old camera. Gran moved a lever and the front panel swung open. The lens

13

popped up on a bracket connected to the back of the camera with black bellows like a concertina. No wonder the leather case was large. The camera looked enormous. Much, much bigger than any *digital* camera he'd ever seen.

His eyes opened wide. He'd forgotten his disappointment over the expensive camera from the park. If he was allowed to use this old camera, it would be like going back in time. But Gran had said cameras like this needed film, and perhaps you couldn't buy film for this camera anymore.

Gran looked at the back where there was a small round red window behind a metal cover. She nodded, as though to herself. Then she looked at Ryan. "There's a film already in here," she said. "The film takes eight black-and-white pictures, as far as I remember, and only two of them have been used up. How very mysterious."

"Black-and-white? That really *is* prehistoric."

Gran smiled. "It can also be artistic."

He held the camera tightly. "Could I ... could I take it to the park and use the rest of the film?" he asked. "And if I get prints made, the mystery of the two pictures will be solved. There might be something really exciting already on it!"

Chapter Four

For the rest of the morning, Ryan spent time searching for things to photograph in the park. Not just any old things, but things that would make *good* photographs in black-and-white. Black-and-white pictures could be artistic, Gran had said. So he would need to find artistic subjects. He didn't want his photographs on the rest of this film to be a boring failure.

He slid the metal cover to reveal the red window. He could see the number 4 now. He'd only taken one picture so far, and he'd even had to remember *to wind the film on by hand*! Gran had insisted she had no idea what was on the first two pictures. The camera hadn't been used for years and years. They were definitely mystery pictures.

There were two dogs that usually jumped and played together at this time of the morning. Were jumping dogs artistic? Anyway, they seemed to be on the autumn half term holiday now — like he was. It was hopeless, Ryan decided, absolutely hopeless to have an old camera like this, a classic probably, and nobody and nothing worthwhile photographing.

His Uncle Jack and family were due from America in the afternoon. There was a photograph of the family on the wall at home. Natalie, his cousin, definitely looked too young to go round with him, but of course the photograph was two or three years old.

He wasn't sure now if he wanted the family from America to come to stay. He'd never met Uncle Jack. Although Uncle Jack was his dad's brother, he was still a stranger, even though his parents sometimes spoke to the family online. Ryan always felt too embarrassed to speak to Natalie, so he kept well out of the way when Skype or FaceTime were mentioned.

To make things worse, he had to sleep down in the front room on a camp bed. The front room wasn't a room he liked very much. It was usually cold and hardly ever used. Uncle Jack and Aunty Lauren would be using his bedroom, although it seemed Uncle Jack would be in London on business most of the time. Natalie — and Ryan had been wondering more each day what Natalie would be like — would have the small spare room. For just a couple of nights that downstairs front room might not be too bad, but for a whole week....

"Let me make sure around your mouth is clean." He just nodded and let his mother check not only his mouth but his ears and neck. To his surprise he passed the test.

"Will you recognise them, Mum?" he asked.

"Only from talking to them online. I've never actually met them. Don't forget, Uncle Jack met Aunty Lauren out in America, before I knew Dad. He's not been back here since."

Ryan and his mother were standing in the upstairs front bedroom that was normally his. It looked so different now with all his things cleared away and an extra bed fitted in. His mother was on tiptoe, peering down the road. His father had driven to the airport. Ryan wanted to go as well, but his father hadn't been sure how much room there would be for the luggage and the family from America.

Then their car drew up outside the house, and Ryan could see his cousin Natalie staring up at him from the back window of the car. She waved. For a moment he didn't want to go downstairs and meet her.

"Come on, Natalie, I'll show you the park."

Natalie nodded. "Race you to the gates," she called, in a voice that sounded strange to Ryan. He hadn't realised she would have an American accent.

And race him she did. Ryan was surprised. The girl stayed in front all the way, her long dark hair streaming out in the wind from under her beanie hat. She was certainly good at running. At the gates she paused to let Ryan catch up.

"It's great here," she panted. "Great. I never thought England would be like this. I was expecting it to be ... well ... I don't know. Anyway, not like this."

Ryan smiled. He wondered what Natalie had been expecting. Perhaps if he went to America he might find it different than he thought. Perhaps Uncle Jack and Aunty Lauren would ask him back to stay with them. He'd met Natalie only half an hour ago, and she seemed easy enough to get on with. He wondered why he'd felt reluctant to see her when she arrived.

"Where does our Gran live?"

Ryan stared. He hadn't really thought of it before. *His* Gran was also *Natalie's* Gran! He could certainly share Natalie with Gran. "Off that long road the other side of the park. Come on, I'll show you. We're all going round to see her after tea, but you and I can be first. Okay?"

Gran was out. Ryan felt disappointed when he got no answer. He wanted to show Natalie all the places and all the people he knew. The old family Bible was in the house.

"There's a key hidden under the tub here. I could show you round the house, but...." Ryan shook his head. "I don't think I'd better. Not until you've met Gran."

"Then you'd better show me the town." Natalie laughed and shook her head to scatter her hair in all directions. "What about the shops?"

"They're okay," Ryan explained, "but I expect you've got all sorts of *enormous* shops in America, like on the films."

"Not where I live," Natalie explained. "I 'spect there are more shops *here* than where *I* live."

As they turned to leave the small terraced house, there was a call from down the road.

"It's Gran!" Ryan shouted. "See? Come on, Natalie, we'll go and help her in with the shopping."

The next hour passed quickly. Natalie got on very well with Gran, and Ryan felt excited to be able to show his American cousin all the things in the house. The old family Bible interested Natalie. She said she couldn't get over the way so many names — including her own — were written in the front pages.

"Your father will remember this old Bible," Gran said to Natalie. "Why not take it back with you now to Ryan's house? You'll be able to look at it together, and make your own copy of all these family names. Some of them go back a hundred and forty years. I'd like you to take a copy of the names to America with you."

"I might be able to photograph them," Ryan explained in excitement. "Gran's got this really old camera. It takes black-and-white photographs and you have to focus the lens and adjust the exposure and things, but you can't see if you got it right until you get the film processed, because there's no screen on the back."

"Who on earth used an old fossil like that?" Natalie asked, laughing.

"Both your fathers did," Gran said, smiling. "But it wasn't new even then. It belonged to your granddad. He bought it new in the 1950s. At that time it was what people now call state-of-the-art. We just called it modern, which of course it was."

"And now we call it a museum piece," Ryan said, laughing. He caught sight of Gran's expression. "I didn't mean to be rude."

She smiled. "That's what we call progress," she said. "You wait, one day all your modern gizmos you think are so amazing will be museum pieces themselves." She winked at Natalie. "Even like old fossils! And when you have grandchildren of your own, you will both probably seem like fossils to them."

"Gran, I'll never think of you as an old fossil," Natalie protested.

"Or even a museum piece," Ryan added, laughing.

Natalie joined Gran in the laughter. "My dad's keen on photography," she said. "He's got a really good camera for photographing these names. We'll be able to print the pages out full size and they'll look just as good as they do here in the old Bible." She started turning over the pages carefully. "Hey, look at all the old engravings in here. They're really old-fashioned, but I think I know all the Bible stories."

Ryan stared at her in amazement. Natalie didn't seem to be boasting. Just stating a fact. He hardly knew any of them himself, but he wasn't letting on. "Are you sure you don't mind us taking it, Gran?"

Ryan received a gentle pat on the head. "No, of course I don't. You'll both look after it, I know."

"I'm sure I will, Gran. And I'm sure Natalie will, too."

Natalie agreed that she definitely would.

"Then you'd better both be getting home. Carry the Bible carefully. The back has come loose. It needs mending."

Ryan and Natalie took turns at holding the Bible as they went down the road. As they reached the corner by the park, Natalie was unable to let go and wave goodbye, in case she dropped it. She just turned and nodded her head and smiled instead.

"Careful as we go across the road," Ryan warmed, realising that Natalie was looking to the left. "The traffic comes the other way in England."

He saw the two motorbikes coming in plenty of time and waited with Natalie on the edge of the pavement.

Ryan felt relieved that he'd thought to warn her. Then he recognised them from the high pitched buzzing sound of the engines. As they got close he knew for sure. It was the bikers who'd tried to take the camera. He relaxed. They wouldn't be interested in the Bible.

Just as the bikes got level with them they stopped, and three youths and a girl all in black motorcycle leathers grinned at them.

The tallest of the four pointed at Ryan. "Why, it's the kid with the expensive camera. I see you've got your girlfriend with you this time."

The others sniggered loudly.

"Do you know them?" Natalie asked.

Ryan shook his head. "I'll tell you later."

The rider pointed to the Bible. "Looks like you've been collecting scrap paper." The dark visor of his helmet stopped Ryan and Natalie seeing his face properly.

Ryan and Natalie stepped back towards the wall, holding the old Bible tightly between them.

"Let's see it, kiddo." The front rider held his hand out towards Ryan. "You don't want to be carrying heavy things like that." The other three riders laughed. "Give it here, see."

Ryan thought of the old family Bible that had been looked after so carefully for a hundred and forty years. Was it going to be taken from them?

"Come on, just a look at the old book." The biker's voice was full of threats. He got off his bike and came across to Ryan and Natalie. The Bible was too heavy to run with, and too precious to leave behind.

The biker pulled it out of their hands. Ryan and Natalie tried to put up a fight but the biker was too tall and strong for them.

"It's an old Bible," the biker jeered, showing it to the others. "What church did you kids steal this from?"

"Give it back," Ryan demanded. "It's an old family Bible. My dad will soon sort you out."

"Oh yes? Your dad and who else?" said the biker with the book.

"His dad and my dad," Natalie said loudly.

"Well we don't think it *is* yours," the rider said, getting back on his machine. "We think you stole it from a church."

Ryan was going to tell them to look in the front at all the family names, but decided to say nothing. They might tear those pages out.

The motorbikes screamed off up the road, the girl on the back holding the Bible above her head. At the far end of the road the bikes turned. The bikers were fooling about, throwing the Bible from one bike to the other.

"Give it back!" Ryan shouted as the bikes shot past. *"Give it back!"*

The bikes came back down the road again. They were coming fast this time. Very fast.

When the bikes were level with Ryan and Natalie, the girl threw the Bible high in the air. The pages opened in the wind. It hit the pavement, bounced, and fell to pieces, its pages and cover scattered along the road. The bikes disappeared round the corner.

Ryan said nothing as he ran to collect as many pages as he could, with Natalie helping. Ryan felt a lump in his throat that wanted to burst out. He held one of the pages in his hand that showed who had been born in the family one hundred and forty years ago. One hundred and forty years! The Bible had been kept carefully for all that time, and now it was wrecked. Surely it could never be put back together.

Several people walking by stopped to help recover every single page. If only they'd been around five minutes ago, this would never have happened! And where was Mr. Stanbury when he was needed?

"Oh, Natalie, what are we going to do?"

Natalie looked as upset as Ryan, but her eyes sparkled. She took her cousin by the arm and held it tightly. "We'll mend it," she announced brightly. "Don't you remember? Gran said it needed mending, anyway! "

Chapter Five

"We're going to the camera shop to get the film developed tomorrow morning, or whatever needs doing to it before we can see the pictures," Ryan announced at Sunday tea the next day. The whole family had gone to church that morning. Rather to Ryan's surprise Natalie had known all the worship songs, and seemed to enjoy being there. "Natalie and I finished the film in the park this afternoon."

He looked across at his mum, full of hope.

"Did you, Ryan?"

He decided his mother hadn't heard properly. He wanted her to offer to pay for the developing and printing. Uncle Jack and his father had gone out for a walk, and Aunty Lauren just carried on with her tea. He couldn't ask his aunt and uncle, anyway. That would seem cheeky.

With Natalie around it had been so much easier to find things to photograph. They'd laid out all the bits of the old family Bible in the garden so they'd have a photograph of how it looked before they began to repair it, even if the photograph wouldn't be very good. Natalie took several with her iPhone — "Just in case," she said with a cheeky grin, without going into details.

"Have it developed, not printed, Ryan." His mother must have heard after all. "You can get the negatives printed later if they're any good."

Ryan nodded. "Will you pay, Mum? Gran says we can still get it done at the camera shop, even though it's an old black-and-white film. Did you know that black-and-white photography is considered special by some people? Perhaps I'll become a famous black-and-white photographer."

"You ask your father about paying to get the film processed. And don't count your chickens before they're hatched. That camera might not be working anymore."

"Even if it isn't, it was probably working when the two mystery photographs were taken."

"Tell that to your father. And don't quote me."

"Thanks, Mum, I'll tell him you said he'd pay!"

His mother raised a finger in caution, but her smile made Ryan realise he was in luck. "Thanks, Mum."

That evening, Natalie and her parents went again to the local church. Ryan explained about the young people's group he went to after the service, but said he'd give it a miss this evening, as was feeling much too tired after being out with the camera.

Natalie said that was a rubbish excuse, because she'd lost several hours' sleep by crossing the Atlantic, and *she* still wanted to go!

Ryan brightened up at that, and went willingly. Even so, he wished he shared Natalie's enthusiasm for hearing more about God.

<><><>

Natalie's father and his own dad left for London early the next morning in the car, and Ryan went with Natalie to the camera shop as soon as it opened. The sign in the window said 1 HOUR PHOTO PRINTING.

The man at the shop smiled when he saw the old camera. "What's this, then?" He laughed gently. "I've not seen one of these for a long time, but I believe they were an expensive model in their day. You didn't get the film from here, did you?"

Ryan explained about his Gran finding the camera in a cupboard, with the film already in it, and two exposures taken. All he and Natalie had done was to use up the rest of the film. That made the young girl assistant come over to see the camera, and she didn't seem at all impressed by it. Ryan decided she knew nothing about photography, and was glad she hadn't been the one to serve them.

The photographer seemed to sense that his assistant had upset Ryan. "Don't underestimate old cameras," he said. "They're like really old motor cars. They don't go like the new models, and they're much more difficult to use. But if you know how to use them, you can get a lot of satisfaction from a vintage car."

"So this is a good camera?" Ryan asked. "A real classic?"

The girl assistant gave a sort of laugh, but covered it up with a cough.

"Can you take the film out, please, and process it?" Ryan wished he'd spent a few minutes at home discovering how to remove the film from the camera, but he knew if he opened the back too soon the light would get onto the film and the pictures would be ruined. He watched carefully now so he wouldn't get caught like this again.

The man removed the roll of film and licked a piece of white tape to stop it unrolling. "Do you want another? I've still got a few in stock." He glanced across at the young assistant and said loudly enough for her to hear, "You're not the only people in town who use film. Several members of the camera club will use nothing but black-and-white film. They think digital cameras take all the skill out of photography. Perhaps they do," he added. "But you can't stop progress. Everyone seems to have a digital camera nowadays."

Except for me, Ryan felt like saying. If his results were as brilliantly artistic as he hoped, his whole future might be in the balance over the next few days. He might become one of the most, perhaps *the* most, famous artistic photographer in the whole world. But then again, perhaps not. "We'll wait to see how this film comes out first."

"That's makes sense. This is a very old film. I must warn you it may not give very good images after such a long time."

"Can you please make negatives out of it?" Ryan asked, remembering what his mum had said. "If anything is worth printing, we can order prints later. Can it be done in one hour, as it says in the window?"

This time the girl gave a more obvious snigger.

The man shook his head. "That's only for digital printing, not films. But after developing the film I'll be able to scan the negatives and make digital prints, if there's anything on the film worth printing."

A faint "If" came from the far end of the shop, followed by another coughing fit.

The man gave Ryan a receipt for the film. "Take no notice of my young assistant," he said. "I'm old enough to remember using film, and the results can be excellent. Tomorrow morning. Any time after nine. The camera club meet here this evening, and I know one of them will process it for you after the meeting."

Natalie came over to the counter. She'd been looking around the shop. "Get another film," she said.

Ryan explained that he wanted to wait, to make sure the camera was working okay.

"It's sure to work," Natalie said confidently.

"Here, I'll buy a film for it myself."

Ryan shrugged. It was his cousin's money, not his. The photographer opened the back of the camera and looked closely into it. He clicked the shutter a few times, changing some of the settings. "I can't guarantee it, but it seems to be working okay. The lens is clear and the focusing moves backwards and forwards as it should do. I can't see any light leaking through the black bellows. But if I were you, I'd wait until you see how this film comes out, and I'll explain how to load it into the camera."

Ryan looked at Natalie and she nodded, obviously agreeing it was a sensible plan. There was no point in wasting money and time if the camera wasn't working properly.

"These old cameras usually go on working for ever," the photographer explained. "But you have to make sure you focus the lens *really* accurately every time you use it, and use this little chart to set the aperture and shutter speed according to the weather conditions."

Ryan just said, "Oh."

"You don't get all this fuss with digital cameras," Natalie said. "You just point and press, no matter what the weather, and everything looks sharp."

"But where's the fun in that?" the photographer asked. "This camera needs a lot more adjusting than the popular digital ones. But get it right, and the results can be superb."

"Only if you get it right," the girl assistant said, loudly enough for Ryan to hear.

Natalie held the old camera as they left the shop. "Well," she announced. "I think it's going to rain soon, so we wouldn't be able to take any more photographs today, even if we bought a film. That man was right, this is fun. I'm sure I'm going to enjoy myself over here. Dad wanted me to go to London with him for a couple of nights while he's on business there."

"What's he doing in London?"

"Mom and dad won't tell me. It's all rather secret. But who wants to go to London? I'd much rather stay here. I can't think London will be as good. Not without you."

Ryan wasn't sure what to say to that, except, "Thanks, I'm glad you didn't go."

<><><>

That afternoon, Natalie sat with Ryan at the large dining table in their Gran's house, with the remains of the Bible spread out on the table and floor. As Natalie had predicted, it was raining quite hard, and she said it felt cosy indoors in England.

"We'll put the pieces of the leather cover over on this side," Natalie said. "I'll try and join them back together. You can sort out the pages."

Ryan held the black leather front cover. "There are some words engraved on here. Right in the middle. In gold." He held it for Natalie to see. "It says, 'Thy Word is a Lamp unto my Feet, and a Light unto my Path.' What does *that* mean?"

Natalie smiled at Ryan's puzzled expression. "It means sort of ... sort of ... well, the Bible is like a light showing us the way."

"The way where?" Ryan asked, frowning.

"The way.... I don't know really." And Natalie laughed.

"That's silly then," Ryan said. "Why put it on the front of a Bible if nobody knows what it means?"

"I'm sure *somebody* knows what it means," Natalie said, taking the front cover from Ryan.

"Oh yes," Ryan agreed, "but I still say it's funny putting something like that on there. Do you think it's a secret message?"

Natalie looked interested at that. "Perhaps there's a secret message hidden in all these family names. They might not be real people at all. Just code words for something else."

Ryan guessed his cousin was joking, but the idea was quite exciting. He had no time for a reply because Gran came into the room.

"How's the repair going? Not finished, have you?"

Ryan and Natalie laughed. As if they *had* finished! It would take hours. *Days!* The table was covered in loose pages. Ryan was glad Gran hadn't blamed them for the disaster. She was only too ready to agree with Natalie's idea that the two of them should try to mend it.

"It's not valuable — just valuable to us. That's because it's been in this family for so long," she'd said. "So it doesn't have to be put back together perfectly. But try and make as good a job of it as you can."

"Natalie thinks there's a secret message in here somewhere," Ryan said, his eyes twinkling in hope. "We can't understand the words on the front cover, so we thought it's a secret message."

Gran leaned over the table. "'Thy Word is a Lamp unto my Feet, and a Light unto my Path.' Why yes, I suppose it is a *sort* of secret message. There are quite a few secret messages in this old Bible."

"Are there, Gran?" Ryan felt really excited. "Can you show them to us?"

"Not yet. You'll have to mend the Bible first. It shouldn't take you long. Most of the pages have stayed together in sections."

"Secret messages," Ryan and Natalie repeated.

Ryan added, "Wow, are they to do with treasure?"

Gran smiled to herself. "I think you could say that. Yes."

Ryan clapped his hands. "Then I'll be able to go for a holiday in America with Natalie. Dad can have a new car, and Mum can——"

"Now just a minute." Ryan felt Gran's hand on his shoulder. "There are many different sorts of treasure. Some treasure doesn't last for very long. And some treasure is worth more than anything in the whole world, but you can't buy things with it. The Bible calls it treasure without price."

Ryan shrugged. He had no idea what Gran was talking about. If it was something to do with treasure, and something to do with what was in this Bible, then it must be some sort of Bible treasure, he decided. Anyway, whatever sort of treasure it was, he wanted his share of it — and some for Natalie, of course.

Chapter Six

The old Bible was slowly getting mended as the evening went on. Natalie proved to be very good at leatherwork, and eventually had the cover sewn back together. Gran had given her a large darning needle and button thread to make sure the hinges stayed firm. Natalie's stitches were rather large, but they didn't look as though they would break free, which was the whole point in sewing it.

Some of the black leather binding had been torn, but Natalie had carefully glued this down, before applying some black shoe polish to the scuff marks, using a soft piece of cloth. Gently, very gently she rubbed at the repairs. Soon the damaged front cover was looking deep black and shiny. Probably better than it had looked for years and years.

Ryan examined it and laughed. "You'll have to do the whole cover now, to make it match! It looks amazing. What do you think, Gran?"

Gran leaned forward and smiled. "Very good. Very good indeed. Come on now, Ryan, you've got a lot more to do, sorting these pages."

Ryan groaned, but he didn't really mind. "What

did you mean about treasure and secret messages?" he asked. He'd been puzzling about that all evening.

"They're all hidden in there," Gran assured him.

"Well," Ryan said, as he put a batch of pages in a neat pile; "well, if you know all this about secret messages and Bible treasure, how come you never found any?"

Her answer surprised both Ryan and Natalie. "I did."

"But you're poor!"

"Ryan!" Natalie sounded shocked.

"Well, not poor," Ryan added, feeling awkward, "but you're not exactly rich are you, Gran?"

Gran didn't seem offended. She laughed at Ryan's puzzled face. "I've got plenty of treasure. As I said, some treasure is worth far more than silver or gold, but you can't buy things with it."

"We sing about that at my church in America," Natalie said.

"Sing what?" Ryan asked, who couldn't remember singing anything about silver and gold at *his* church.

"We sing, 'I'd rather have Jesus than silver or gold', but I can't remember how it goes on. I think it's a really old hymn."

Gran smiled at Natalie. "There's a real treasure trail in this Bible. Read out the words on the front cover again."

Natalie stopped her polishing and read, "'Thy

Word is a Lamp unto my Feet, and a Light unto my Path.' Is that from the Bible? Is that why it's there?"

"It's from the longest chapter in the whole Bible. Psalm one hundred and nineteen. Round about verse one hundred, I think."

Ryan felt interested. "So how's that a clue to the treasure trail?"

"Imagine a bright flashlight — but don't stop your working, either of you. That light is like God's word, the Bible. Like that bright flashlight it will help you find your way in the dark. It will show you which way the path goes. If there's anything in the way you'll see it before you trip over it."

"And it will frighten scary things away," Natalie added.

"Is that what the Bible does?" Ryan asked. "Frighten scary things away?"

Gran nodded. "If you read it, but not if you keep it closed. That's like having a flashlight you never switch on in the dark."

"I think there's a lot in the Bible about light," Natalie said.

"You're quite right, love. The verse on the cover is only the start of the treasure trail. The first clue, in a way."

Ryan felt impatient. "Give us some more clues, please, Gran."

"Well, in John chapter one you'll find out about an even brighter light. With those two lights you'll have all you need to find your way through life to the treasure."

"So we read the Bible, and find what? The treasure?" Ryan asked.

"You'll have to get the Bible stuck back together to find more about it."

"Oh, Gran," Ryan pleaded, "tell us more about it!"

"No, I've told you quite enough for you to take in for the moment. Come on, if you sit staring into space you'll never get finished."

"Yes, come on, Ryan," Natalie chided him. "You're holding the job up."

Ryan grinned. "Give me a hand with these pages, then. You'll polish the cover away if you're not careful!"

<><><>

Ryan woke up full of hope. The film would be ready at the camera shop today. He felt excited to see how the pictures had come out, or indeed if they'd come out at all. He wasn't quite sure what negatives would look like.

Black-and-white photography was supposed to be artistic. Maybe with this camera he could take some photographs for an exhibition somewhere. When he grew up he might become internationally famous for his artistic black-and-white snaps — no, not snaps, photographs. Images, even. On this film there might already be some of his own photographs that would start him on his road to fame. Or more likely, there would be nothing worth printing, apart from the two mystery photographs.

The man behind the counter at the camera shop was just opening up when Ryan and Natalie got there. He retrieved a packet from a shelf at the back and handed it over with a smile. The girl assistant wasn't at the counter. Ryan was glad. That man had been pleasant and enthusiastic about the camera. If the film hadn't come out, she would probably be even ruder than she was yesterday!

Ryan paid, and the man laid some large strips of film onto a lightbox so they could see the results. There were grey and white shapes on all the pieces of film, but they didn't look much like proper pictures.

The photographer explained that he had another customer to serve. He gave them a powerful magnifying glass and told them he'd be back as soon as he was free.

"What are these?" Ryan asked Natalie in astonishment.

"I suppose they're negatives." Natalie didn't seem to know any more about photography than he did.

Ryan peered through the magnifying glass. "This one is of you, Natalie. I think I was too close. It looks so fuzzy."

"Everything looks wrong. Why is my face dark

and my hair so white?"

Ryan frowned. "The dark things are light, and the light things are dark. I think that's how negatives are. The picture of the old family Bible in pieces is *really* fuzzy. I didn't understand about focusing. Lucky for us your iPhone pictures are so clear. It's good to have a record of all our hard work."

"Who's this?"

Ryan looked at the negative his cousin was pointing to. "I didn't take it. It's a boy. It's definitely not me. I'd never wear a long coat with a belt like *that*!"

The negative showed a boy standing under a tree.

"And who's this, Ryan?"

The tree was the same, but the boy was smaller.

"I didn't take that one, either. What's going on?"

Natalie laughed. "You said two of the pictures had already been taken. These are the first two exposures on the film. Got it?"

"Then who are the two boys?"

"Simple," Natalie said. "I know who they are."

"Who?"

"Guess."

"Can't."

"Think of two men who were boys once."

"All men were boys once ... I suppose," Ryan said, frowning. "Come on, who are——? Hey, I know! Your dad and mine! They must have been taken *years* ago."

"You said the film was old."

"Well, just wait till we show them these negatives."

Natalie caught hold of Ryan's arm, and put a finger to her lips. "Let's make it a secret."

"What on earth for?" Ryan decided his American cousin was too fond of secrets.

"No one knows about this but us. Right?"

"Right."

"We could get these negatives printed and put into frames. Then we can give them as a present to Gran."

"What a great idea. A present for Gran. We can take some black-and-white photos of ourselves with the old camera, and frame them as well. Yes, you're right," Ryan agreed; "we'll keep it a secret."

Natalie pointed to the film on the lightbox. "Let's leave these two negatives for printing now. The rest look a bit rubbish anyway."

Ryan was examining the negatives again. "The others *do* look a bit fuzzy, but they may not be all *that* rubbish. We can ask what the man thinks about the pictures of us. Perhaps they'll look all right when they're printed."

"No they won't!" Natalie said firmly. "If you're going to frame a picture of me, I want to look my best."

Ryan rolled his eyes. "Okay, then we'll buy another film for the camera. We know we have to focus it much more carefully now. Black-and-white of course. We need to take some artistic photographs."

"Well, give me plenty of warning if you're going to take one of me. Anyway, what's the difference between ordinary photographs and artistic ones?"

"Well, ordinary photographs are just snapshots with the person standing to attention and grinning at the camera. And artistic ones are...?"

"Yes?"

"Well ... artistic. Sort of different. Good enough to put in a magazine, and everyone goes ooooh when they see them!"

Natalie gave a cheeky grin. "And in focus."

Ryan nodded. "Yes, that probably helps."

The man had finished with his customer and came back to the counter. Ryan explained what was wanted.

The photographer looked at the first two negatives. "Yes, they should print all right. They're a bit faint. That's because the film is long out of date. They could have been worse. Has the film been kept in the cold?"

Ryan smiled. "It's been in the camera in my Gran's house. She always says her house is the coldest one in the whole country! "

The photographer laughed. "That may be bad

for her, but it's been good for the film. These two pictures aren't bad. Not bad at all."

Ryan waited for the man to say that the others were hopelessly bad, but he said nothing about them. Ryan felt proud that two were okay. Then he realised he couldn't take the credit. The photographs had been taken long before he was born. They'd been lying hidden on the film and nobody knew anything about them. Even his Gran had no idea what the two pictures were of.

"I'll scan the negatives, and run them through Photoshop. That will brighten them up. No extra charge. You can have prints by lunchtime. I have some other scanning to do as soon as my young assistant gets in. Any particular size?"

Ryan hoped the "young assistant" would be late today, and not in time to see his fuzzy negatives.

Natalie had been examining the display of photo frames. There was one in natural wood that was rather like the cover of a book. It opened up, and on each side there was a space for a photograph. "We'd like to put them in here."

Ryan saw the price. "Are you sure, Nat? I haven't got much money."

The man seemed extremely interested in the conversation. "You ... you will be able to ... er, pay for the two prints and the frame, I hope."

Natalie produced a small wallet from her bag and opened it to show the man the contents. Ryan tried to look but was unable to see his cousin's great wealth — or lack of it! However, the photographer seemed satisfied. Natalie closed her wallet with a snap. She turned to Ryan.

"Don't be nosey," she said. "And don't call me Nat."

Ryan shrugged. Why should he care how much money his cousin had, anyway?

"Please will you put the frame to one side for us," Natalie said. "And another film please." She opened her wallet again. "You said you kept some black-and-white films for the camera club. How much are they?"

Natalie paid for the film. The packaging said 120 ROLL FILM. Ryan asked the photographer to load it into the camera, just to be sure it was done correctly. He didn't think he'd need any more films, but it was just as well to know how to do it.

With the camera loaded and safely back in its brown leather case, he and Natalie left the shop.

"Oh, brighten up," Natalie said as soon as they were outside. "Call me Nat if you like. It's just that nobody ever does. Yes, I rather like it when you call me that."

Ryan did brighten up. He was glad his American cousin was staying here. He'd call her Nat if she wanted him to. He hadn't realised he'd done it in the shop. There was one thing though. Was Natalie's family ever so rich? Certainly Natalie had her own iPhone and all sorts of other bits and pieces of her own. He smiled to himself. How much money *did* Natalie have in the small purse she called a wallet?

Chapter Seven

Immediately after leaving the camera shop, Natalie went with Ryan to the park. Ryan told her she was far too fussy about how she looked in the photos, but Natalie just laughed.

"It's my camera," Ryan warned her.

"It's Gran's camera, and it's my film."

Ryan could think of nothing to say in reply to that.

"Anyway," Natalie said, "we can always use my iPhone and take some photos and get them printed at the camera shop. The camera works every time, no matter whether it's sunny or dark. We can take some selfies, and if I don't like them I can just delete them."

Ryan felt upset now. He'd only been joking with his cousin.

Natalie laughed again. "Don't look like that, Ryan. I like Gran's old camera. Besides, without it, we wouldn't have found the pictures of our dads when they were boys. If we can get good photos of each other with it, they'll go with the two of our dads in another frame. A sort of matching set taken with the same camera. I'm sure Gran would like that."

Ryan could see what Natalie meant. It *was* an old camera, but nowadays it seemed quite special because it *was* so old. That photographer was quite right when he said it was like a vintage car. It might not go as well a modern one, and as he'd discovered it was much more difficult to use. But in a way that was part of the appeal. And it worked well enough for them to mess about with. If Natalie wanted to be photographed looking her best, then he would see what he could do.

"Hey, it's those two kids again!"

Ryan and Natalie turned in surprise.

"Where did you steal the camera from, kids? A museum?"

Two motorbikes were resting outside the park gates and two bikers were sitting on the grass just inside. Their helmets were by them on the grass. They were definitely part of the four who had thrown the Bible in the air and wrecked it.

"Hurry up," Natalie said urgently to Ryan. "Let's get home before they do any more harm."

Ryan shook his head. "I want a photograph of them. Then we'll be able to find out who they are. Get your phone out. I haven't got mine with me, anyway."

Natalie shook her head. "They're watching us. They'll take my phone and smash it if they see what we're doing."

Ryan had a plan. Hadn't he been told he was the best runner in his class at school? And it seemed Natalie was even faster! "Give me your phone then, Nat. I don't want you getting hurt."

Natalie shook her head. "I'm more bothered about my phone than about me. Use Gran's old camera. Take the picture and we'll run as fast as we can back to yours. But why don't we just write down the bike licence plates?"

"I'd rather have a photo of those two," Ryan said. "We want to show their faces, not their bikes."

"Then you'd better hurry. They're getting up."

Ryan felt a chill of excitement running through him. The two bikers began walking across in their direction. Had they guessed what was happening? He opened up the old camera and set it for a cloudy day. That should do it. It was too soon to take the photo yet. They would have to be a lot closer before they'd come out clearly on the photo.

"Been robbing the museum?" The larger of the two was wearing black motorcycle leathers.

"Tut, tut. First you rob the church, and then the museum." The second biker had black curly hair and wore blue denim jeans.

Ryan felt furious. He didn't look through the viewfinder. That would give the game away. He set the focus for ten feet, held the camera steady and squeezed the shutter.

The click sounded ever so loud to him. The

bikers must have heard.

"Let's see it then." The first biker held out his hand as he got close.

Ryan looked at Natalie and together they turned and ran — back into the park and towards the gate on the far side.

The two bikers started to run after them and then returned to their bikes.

Ryan grinned all over his face. "Easy," he announced. "I told you we'd get away from them."

Natalie grinned too. "How about taking my photo, then?"

Ryan shook his head. "No fear. Not now. I want to get out of here and as far away as we can. We'll come back this afternoon."

A surprise was waiting for them at the far gates. The two bikers were sitting on their motorcycles. "That was rude to run away," the one in blue jeans told them. "We don't like rude kids. And we don't like having our photograph taken."

"It was your fault," Ryan shouted at him. "You started it!"

"Well, we're going to have to teach you a lesson."

"Just try!" Ryan called, as he and Natalie turned and ran.

"We can't get away," Natalie gasped as they paused for breath by the small ornamental pond. There were plenty of trees and bushes for cover, even though they were losing their leaves, but only the two gates out. One of the bikers had already ridden round to guard the other gate. They were trapped — in an empty park!

"We'll just have to wait here until somebody comes," Ryan said. "Our dads are in London, and it's no good phoning Mum." He didn't like the way the two bikers had threatened to get them. Natalie didn't seem frightened, but perhaps she just wasn't showing it.

"We'll go into the bushes here and hide. Okay, Nat?"

The bushes still had enough leaves to give good cover. After a few minutes Ryan decided it was safe to look out. He came back to report to Natalie.

"I can see one of them by the far gates, but no one this side. Come on, let's make a run for it."

"Not run. Just creep quietly. I learnt some tricks from the Native American Indians."

"From *real* ones?"

"Of course. They live all round us in America." Natalie looked at Ryan, then burst out laughing. "I've never seen a real one in my life, but I've seen them on a film on the telly."

"So have I," Ryan said, "but never in the park like this!"

There was the sound of a motorbike revving up. Ryan and Natalie were in the open now.

"We'll just have to stay here," Ryan said quietly.

"They'll never come in after us. Not with their bikes. You can't bring any sort of bike in here."

How wrong he was. The two riders signalled to each other across the park. There was a high pitched buzz from their engines and the two bikes shot across the grass, throwing up mud and leaves as they skidded to a halt beside Ryan and Natalie.

"Just give me the camera. We know you've got a photograph of us on there."

Ryan held it behind his back.

"Come on, kid, do as he says." The second rider spoke now.

"You'd better get your bikes out of here. You'll be in trouble," Ryan warned them.

"Oh, we will, will we? Then you'd better give us the camera or *you'll* be in trouble."

Ryan and Natalie ran, chased by the two bikes. A woman and a man with a dog had come into the park, but they just stood and stared. Everything was going wrong. Ryan slipped and fell. The camera tumbled across the grass. The biker in black leathers rode by quickly, circled the camera and came by more slowly. He reached down and picked it up.

"Thanks, kid!"

He opened the camera and ripped out the film, leaving it hanging from the back. Then the game with the old family Bible was repeated, but without the girl and the other biker. The two bikers rode round the park, over the grass, throwing the camera from one to the other, the film streaming out behind. The woman and the man with the dog continued to stand and watch.

Ryan looked in horror as his camera was thrown high in the air over one of the bushes. Just behind the bush was the small pond. To his relief the camera stopped at the edge.

The bikes were tearing pieces out of the grass. The riders seemed unable to find the camera. Ryan stayed where he was. He certainly wasn't going to help them!

One bike fell over by the pond, but the rider quickly jumped on again. His leathers were muddy from the damp earth, and his bike didn't sound quite as healthy as he revved the engine.

"Get in the bushes here," Natalie hissed.

Ryan and Natalie hid again. The bikes did one quick circuit of the park, then screamed off down the road. The woman and the man were standing quite close to the bush as Ryan and Natalie crawled out. The coast seemed to be clear.

The woman looked at them closely. "Well, really!" she scolded. *"Whatever* were you all playing at?"

"Not us," Ryan said indignantly. "It wasn't us. It was those two on the bikes."

The woman didn't seem to be listening. "I've a good mind to take you both down to the police station. Fancy damaging a lovely park like this! "

Natalie went wild. "How could it have been us?" she screamed. "Can we ride motorbikes?"

Ryan looked round for the man with the dog, but he'd disappeared.

"You young hooligans," the woman said. "And don't you be cheeky to me, young lady."

Natalie calmed down a little. "If you *know* who they are, then go and tell the police. We'll come with you!"

But she was wasting her breath. The woman had stormed off.

Ryan went to fetch the camera. The coil of film hung from the back. The light would have ruined the photos.

"It's no good," he called, showing the camera to Natalie. "I don't think we'll *ever* catch them."

Natalie took the camera from Ryan and examined it closely. "It's only the back that's come open. I think it still works okay. We've only lost the film. We can buy another. I'm glad we didn't use my phone. They'd probably have taken it with them. Don't worry, we'll *definitely* catch them!"

Chapter Eight

The photographer was surprised to find Ryan and Natalie back in the shop so soon. "I'm afraid your prints won't be ready until after lunch," he said. "I've had a busy morning. My young assistant hasn't come in today. Sorry."

Ryan thought it was good news that the "young assistant" wasn't around, and Natalie put on her best smile. "That's all right," she said. "We want another film, please."

"What, another one already?" The man sounded surprised.

Natalie grinned. She had a friendly way of grinning that seemed to make her friends with everyone immediately. Ryan, on the other hand, knew he was always slower to get to know people. He was never quite sure what people would think of him.

"It was spoilt," Natalie said. "So was the camera — nearly!"

Ryan hoped they wouldn't have to explain. It still made him mad to think of those two youths on their motorbikes. He put the camera on the counter. The black leather on the camera body was now clean of mud from the park, and nothing had been bent out of shape. The shutter still clicked, and the lens looked undamaged. He was relieved that the biker had only opened the back.

Once again Natalie was the one who had to pay. "Thanks," she said as the man handed the camera back. "See you later in the morning for another film!" And she laughed.

The photographer laughed too, and Ryan wished he could make jokes so easily. Natalie seemed to find it easy to talk with everyone. If he joked like this he would probably sound rude.

Natalie had been rude though, he remembered — in the park to that woman by the pond. Natalie had shouted at her most rudely. And the woman hadn't liked it. Ryan wondered whether she would go round to his house and complain. Oh well, he thought to himself, she probably had no idea where he lived.

"Come on," Natalie called from the shop door. "Don't stand there in a dream!"

Ryan thanked the photographer and joined his cousin on the pavement outside the shop. It was sunny now — just the sort of day for taking pictures.

"The park," Ryan announced. "We'll make for the park again. I 'spect the sun will be bright enough for our old camera."

"*Gran's* camera," Natalie corrected him.

Ryan looked surprised. "Did I say 'our' camera? Well, I think Gran means us to keep it. Anyway, you bought the film, both times. Race you to the park gates!"

This time Ryan was quite a bit in the lead as they came round the corner and into the road by the park. Luckily Ryan was able to stop quickly. Natalie saw her cousin stop and guessed something was happening. She crept the last few yards and stood close behind Ryan.

"What's up?"

"Those two bikes. They're the same bikes, aren't they?'

"They sure look like them," Natalie agreed. "Let's go a bit closer. There's no one with them. Coming?"

Ryan shook his head. "No fear! Not after what happened just now."

"Oh come on," Natalie said. "We'll creep like Native American Indians again."

"A lot of good that did us last time," Ryan reminded her.

"There they are!" Natalie almost shouted in excitement. "See? Down by the pond. They're looking for something. Perhaps a part of the bike got knocked off when it fell."

Two bikers, and a girl this time, all carrying helmets, were examining the pond and poking into the soft mud with sticks.

"Let's get closer," Natalie said, "I want to copy down the licence plates of those bikes."

"Going to tell the police?" Ryan asked, feeling excited.

Natalie shook her head. "Not yet. I doubt there's much the police could do. Besides, they must have damaged one of their bikes when it fell. Perhaps they've learned a lesson."

Perhaps they had, Ryan thought, but he doubted it. He'd come to dislike those bikers very much, and he didn't even know them!

Natalie was carrying a shoulder bag which, much to Ryan's surprise she called her purse. Her purse was definitely the small thing she kept her money in — the thing she called her wallet. Things seemed to be called by strange names in America.

Natalie got out a pen and notebook and copied the licence numbers from the two bikes. Ryan checked them and nodded. Natalie was just closing her bag when they heard voices behind. The bikers and the girl were coming. They could either run, or stay where they were by the bushes.

Natalie held tightly to Ryan's arm. "Just look the other way and they mightn't see us."

Ryan had to agree. To run now would only attract attention. Slowly he leaned forward and hid the camera in the branches of the bush. At least *that* would be safe!

"Dead easy!" one of the bikers was saying.

"Well, I'm a bit scared," the girl said. They were talking loudly and seemed to have no idea Ryan and Natalie were listening.

"Yer, dead easy," the first biker repeated. "It will be the easiest job we've ever done. Plenty of money for us, too."

"Sounds okay," the second one agreed. "This evening."

"Yer, seven o'clock. Think of all that money!"

The others laughed. The girl stood thoughtfully by the bike. "Yeah, money just waiting for us. I hope we'll be all right."

The others looked at her in surprise. "All right?" the first biker asked. "All right? You're nuts, girl. Of course we will. There's nothing to go wrong. We'll meet outside at seven tonight. At the top of the steps. We need to stick together."

The three got onto the bikes. "Seventeen steps!" the rider on front called to the others. "Seventeen steps to a load of money!"

"A load of money," the other biker called, and this made the others laugh again. "We're going to be rich!"

The bike engines started, and Ryan and Natalie were left by the bushes along the edge of the park.

"Wow!" Natalie said as soon as the bikes were out of sight. "What a smashing holiday! They're a gang of robbers. A load of money, they said."

"But where?" Ryan asked. "They said they were

going to do a job and it was dead easy."

"Seventeen steps. Is there a bank in town called Seventeen Steps?"

Ryan laughed. "Nothing like it. Anyway, I think that he meant the money was *down* seventeen steps."

"Who'd leave money at the bottom of seventeen steps?" Natalie asked.

Ryan felt excited. "This evening!" He could imagine a dark alleyway, seventeen steps down to some basement, and money wrapped in a parcel waiting to be stolen. He told Natalie about it. To his surprise she didn't laugh.

"Let's catch them at it," he said excitedly.

"Where? Where are there seventeen steps?"

Ryan shook his head. "I can't think, unless....."

"Yes?" Natalie asked impatiently.

"Down near the shops. There's a row of old houses with basements, and steps down to them from the pavement. Some of them are ever so dark and creepy. Jake who does odd jobs around our way says wealthy people are squatting in some of them."

Natalie laughed. "Wealthy squatters? Whoever heard of *wealthy* squatters?"

Ryan shrugged, and tried to sound mysterious. "Ah, that's it. They've got so much money they have to pretend they haven't got any."

"Why?"

"So they won't get robbed. Whoever would

think to rob them?"

"I certainly wouldn't," Natalie agreed.

"Nor would anyone else. So there they all are, living in the basements of Armitage Terrace, with bags of money containing thousands of pounds. A lot of them are really old, and they're afraid to take it to the bank in case it gets stolen on the way, and they're afraid to leave it in the house if they go out. So they have to stay indoors all the time and guard it."

"Where's Armitage Terrace?" Natalie asked, wondering whether to believe a single word her cousin was telling her. She'd been going to laugh, but Ryan seemed serious.

"Hundreds of thousands of pounds," Ryan said, trying to hide a smile. It seemed Natalie would believe anything! "We've got to warn them, and keep guard."

"I'm not going down to any basements to guard their money," Natalie protested, "so you'll be going by yourself."

"I'm not saying it *is* Armitage Terrace," Ryan explained. "It just *may* be. Let's go and see how many steps there are down to the basements. If there aren't exactly seventeen, then we'll know the robbery won't be there."

Natalie agreed to this. Ryan assured her that Armitage Terrace wasn't far away. Picking the camera out of its hiding place in the bush, the two cousins made their way towards the edge of town.

"Is this it?" Natalie asked in surprise. "It's not very ... er, special, is it!"

Armitage Terrace certainly wasn't very special. A hundred years ago it might have been. Now there were boarded-up windows and cracked walls on houses that were once so grand. Just a few of the houses were still lived in, although these were few and far between.

"They'll be knocking them all down soon," Ryan explained. "They're going to do something with this road, but I'm not sure what. It was on the local news."

"It's horrid!" Natalie said with a shudder. "Imagine coming here after dark. I'm off!"

Ryan held onto her arm. "Come on, you promised."

"Promised what?"

"Promised to count the steps."

Natalie shook her head. "I don't remember. You count them if you want to."

Ryan sighed. "You stay at the top. Okay?"

Natalie agreed, but told Ryan to hurry. The first house had no way down to the basement. The second seemed to be lived in, but the third was just right. The old iron gate at the top of the steps was open. The windows and door at the bottom were boarded up, and no one could live there. It would be safe to count the steps without anyone seeing.

Ryan stood at the top of the steps and tried to count, but every time he tried he got a different answer. There was nothing for it but to go down. He now felt far from brave and wished Natalie could be with him. Although it was mid-morning, it was so gloomy he almost needed a light. He could see now what that verse on the cover of the Bible meant. At times like this you needed some sort of special light to show you the way.

"Hurry up!" Natalie called, from where she was peering through a gap in the railings.

"All right, I'm going as fast as I can. I don't want to slip."

Ryan made his way to the bottom. He'd only been joking with Natalie about the wealthy squatters, but this was suddenly very scary. It might even be true! The daylight above seemed to disappear. Twelve, thirteen, fourteen. That felt like the bottom now. Yes, one of the boarded up windows was in front of him. Could there be three more steps anywhere? He made his way slowly round the corner. There could be three more steps down to a coalhouse or something.

It was ever so quiet. The high wall up to the pavement cut out all the noise of the traffic. Ryan was completely alone. Or was he?

From inside the house came a rattling sound. The basement door opened a bit. Ryan jumped. A face covered in whiskers and dirt appeared in the doorway and then the door slammed shut — hard!

"Clear off!"

Ryan moved like lightning. In seven quick strides, taking the steps two at a time, he was at the top with Natalie.

"You came up a bit fast," Natalie said in surprise.

"That was scary," Ryan said breathlessly, looking pale. He peered cautiously over the railings. "Really, *really* scary!"

Chapter Nine

"Fourteen steps," Ryan said. "Definitely only fourteen. Besides," he laughed, "I wouldn't go down there again, even if there *were* seventeen!"

Natalie, who had heard about the face in the doorway, agreed with her cousin. "So if there are only fourteen steps at this house, they'll all be the same in every house in this road, won't they, Ryan?"

Ryan said he was sure they would. *Absolutely* sure they would. "It's hopeless," he admitted. "There are probably thousands of places with seventeen steps, and we'll never find one of them. Let's go back to the park and I'll take your photo standing by the pond. And then you can take one of me."

Natalie looked at Ryan and laughed. "It's a good thing the film is in black-and-white. You look ever so pale!"

Ryan felt cross, but he tried not to show it.

"When will those prints of our dads be ready at the camera shop?" he asked, changing the subject.

Natalie looked excited. "Lunchtime, he said. If we go round now we'll only have to wait a few minutes."

Ryan held the camera against his waist and pointed it at Natalie. "Smile, please!" He laughed, then pressed the shutter.

"Now why did you go and do that?" Natalie demanded. "I wanted to look my best."

Ryan laughed again and ran ahead of Natalie. Turning round, he called, "If we go through the park I'll take some more."

Natalie gave chase.

It was well after twelve when they finally got to the shop. The new film had been used up by the pond in the park — mostly of Natalie! She'd been so sure that in each one she'd either shut her eyes or not looked "quite right." Ryan had made do with just one exposure of himself.

Soon the photographer was writing out the order for developing the latest film, and no prints yet. He said he liked to encourage young photographers, and would scan the negatives and they could see them on the monitor in the shop in the morning, and choose which ones they wanted printing. Then he looked in the box of completed orders and took out a large envelope.

"Here you are," he said. "Two prints for framing, hot off the printer."

Natalie nodded, and she and Ryan watched as the man opened the envelope. The two black-and-white pictures of their dads weren't quite as good as Ryan had hoped, but Natalie seemed pleased. Then

Ryan looked again, and decided they were good after all.

The "young assistant" was in the shop now and she came across to be nosey.

"They're our dads," Natalie explained to her.

"Bit young to be parents, aren't they?" she said.

Ryan and Natalie laughed, and so did the photographer. The "young assistant" went back to whatever she'd been doing at the other end of the shop. Surely she'd been joking. Ryan saw how red her face had gone. So perhaps not.

"And the frame like this you put aside for us, please," Natalie said, pointing to the display of the book-shaped frames she'd seen the day before. "Can you show us how to fit the photos in, please?"

While the photographer was fitting the photographs into the double frame, Natalie explained how they were going to give them as a surprise present to their Gran.

"Her birthday?" the photographer asked.

"No," Natalie said, "just a surprise present. Presents aren't a surprise on a birthday, because you're expecting them. If you get one on an ordinary day it *must* be a surprise present."

Ryan looked at Natalie. That was one of the nicest ideas he'd ever heard. A surprise present on an ordinary day when you weren't expecting anything. He would try to find Natalie a surprise present before she went back to America. But what?

It would be no good asking her, because she'd guess what he was planning to do. He must remember when she said she liked something she saw, and try and buy it for her secretly. Well, he thought, he'd have to hurry, because Natalie and her parents would be returning to America in three more days.

"What a thoughtful pair you both are," the man said. "Did you think of this by yourselves?"

"She thought of it." Ryan nodded towards his cousin. "And she's going to pay 'cos I've got no money."

Natalie opened her wallet. "He's going to pay me back half one day, but he doesn't know it," she said.

"I will, Nat," Ryan promised. "Honest I will."

The photographer had fitted the photos into the folding frame by this time and Ryan suddenly appreciated just how good they looked. Black-and-white photography *could* be artistic. Maybe the ones by the pond of Natalie would be artistic, too. The frame Natalie had chosen had a sort of old-fashioned look which suited the photos. To show their fathers as boys, the pictures must have been taken *ages* ago.

"That's *your* dad, Nat."

"How do you know?"

Ryan and Natalie were standing on the pavement outside the shop. The photographer would probably have talked for longer, but there were other customers to see to.

"He's younger, Nat. Your dad is younger than mine. Look at the trees in the background. These two photos must have been taken at the same time. See?"

Natalie patted Ryan on the back. "Quite a ... what's his name ... Sherlock Holmes?"

"Just my brilliant brain," Ryan said.

Natalie laughed. "Well then, brilliant brain, just find the seventeen steps where those bikers are going to get all that money at seven. That will show me how brilliant you are."

"Even the best brains need resting," Ryan said. "It's your turn to do some thinking now."

"It might be *upstairs* somewhere," Natalie said thoughtfully. "The seventeen steps could go *up.*"

Ryan shook his head. "They said they'd meet at the top of the steps and then go *down.*"

"You're right," Natalie agreed. "Seventeen steps. Seventeen steps. It sounds to me a bit like the name of a restaurant or club."

Ryan stood and stared at Natalie. "Could be," he said slowly. "Not that I've ever heard of it. We can't go all over the city looking for a place called the Seventeen Steps."

"Not by seven o'clock tonight, Ryan. They said they were meeting to do the job at seven. What could we do, anyway, if we got there?"

"Just be there," Ryan said. "Just be there and watch."

"And try and stop them, if we can," Natalie added. "Or phone the police. Anyway, I'm hungry. Let's go back for lunch. We can make our plans for this afternoon after we've eaten. A top secret meeting in your room. Okay?"

Ryan decided lunch was one of the most sensible suggestions he'd heard for a long time.

"What about the photos?" he asked, holding the camera shop bag up to Natalie. "When do we give them to Gran?"

Natalie held a finger to her lips. "That's another secret," she said. "We've got to wait until the pictures of *us* are ready."

"But that will be tomorrow," Ryan said with a groan. "First the photographer has to get the film developed and then we have to choose the best negatives for printing. He may not be able to print them straight away. I can't wait that long."

Natalie said she didn't think she could either. "Not yet, though," she warned. "The first thing we have to do is plan where we're going to find these seventeen steps."

Ryan caught hold of Natalie's arm. "Get your phone out. We'll do a search on the internet."

Natalie got online and began typing in the search box.

"Put the name of our town as well," Ryan said,

and from the look on Natalie's face, he decided he'd probably insulted her by saying something so obvious. Insulted or not, she keyed in the town and pressed *search*.

"Seventeen Steps Restaurant and Club!" Ryan looked over Natalie shoulder and read the name out in excitement. "There's their phone number. Let's warn them they're going to be raided at seven o'clock this evening?"

Natalie shook her head. "They wouldn't believe us. We'll do what you said. We'll go and keep guard. Do you know where it is?"

Ryan looked closely at the address. "I think so. Walton Street. It's across town. Click their website and bring up the map. I'll be able to find it," he assured Natalie.

Natalie shivered in excitement. "What an adventure this is going to be," she said. "Come on, we'll go to your room and make our plans!"

Chapter Ten

"I don't think we ought to go there without telling anyone," Natalie said, curling up on Ryan's folding bed in the downstairs front room. Ryan sat on the carpet. They'd eaten their lunch and come straight to the room for their meeting.

"We can't tell our dads, because they've gone to London. And my mum can't drive us to the Seventeen Steps because Dad's taken the car," Ryan said. In a way he was glad. To have shared their secret might have been a bad thing. At least they'd be able to have their adventure alone.

Seven o'clock. It wasn't very late really. If it all came to nothing, they could be on the bus and back home well before eight. And if they stopped the robbery and the bikers were caught, they'd be heroes, and it wouldn't matter what time they got home.

"We'll have to ask," Natalie said. "I don't want to go out without saying anything."

"But they might stop us," Ryan protested. By "they" he meant their mothers.

"Then we can't go," Natalie said.

Ryan wasn't surprised by Natalie's answer.

There was something about her that made her just that little bit different. Sure, she liked to go running with him and have secrets just like anyone else. It was something about the way she behaved. Sometimes she got cross, sometimes angry, and yet…. Then there was the Bible by her bed. Natalie seemed to have found out more about this "light" business than he had.

"Nat," he said slowly, lying on his back on the floor and staring up at the ceiling. "Nat, are you ever so religious?"

His cousin laughed. "Yes, that's why I carry a little bell and go round chanting all day long!"

"No, Nat, be sensible. You know, do you pray a lot and that sort of thing?"

Natalie nodded. "A bit. It's just that Jesus is my friend, so…."

"You *friend*!" Ryan said. "You mean like *I'm* your friend?"

"Yep, in a way. Like now. I'm enjoying talking to you, but I don't mind who knows we're talking together. And I don't mind who knows I talk to Jesus. See?"

"I 'spose so. How come Jesus is your friend?"

"I asked him to be," Natalie said simply.

"I don't think I'd dare," Ryan said. "Not till I'm older. When I'm older, I expect I'll be a better sort of person."

"It's not like that really," Natalie said. "Jesus

sort of puts you right. He doesn't make you perfect, but you want to be. And he forgives you for all the things you've done wrong, so God won't punish you."

Ryan looked at Natalie to see if she was serious. She was. Even though he went to church, he knew he hadn't thought about Jesus very much before. Whatever had happened to Natalie certainly seemed good. Knowing that she had Jesus as her friend seemed to make her a brighter, more ... well, different person, in a good way. Ryan wished he could ask her more, but he didn't want to let on that he couldn't really understand what she meant. Perhaps if he tried hard enough....

"You don't try, you just have to ask," Natalie explained, as though reading his thoughts. "I can't put it any better than that. Gran would know what I mean."

Ryan nodded. He reckoned she would.

Then quite suddenly he changed the subject. He couldn't tell why, but he suddenly began to feel uncomfortable.

"It's too far to walk, but I know which bus to get," he told her.

"Okay, but we'll have to say where we're going, and why. That's definite." Natalie sounded as though her mind was made up.

"Oh, no, please don't tell them *everything*. Let's tell them we want to go to the shops. The big stores are open in the evening."

Natalie wouldn't give in. "We can't just sneak off. We'd be in terrible trouble if we got found out."

All of a sudden Ryan was glad Natalie had spoken out. He'd begun to feel the same way himself. There was no need to tell the whole of their secret. Just enough about the bus journey to get permission.

Ryan and Natalie found their mothers sitting in the kitchen. They were drinking tea.

"Mum," Ryan said, trying not to sound too eager. "Mum, do you know the Seventeen Steps in Walton Street?"

His mother put her cup down, thought for a minute and then said, "Seventeen Steps? I've heard of it. It's a sort of club and restaurant. They have live music. The place hasn't been open long. We pass close to Walton Street on the way to Aunty Debbie's place. Why are you asking? Not thinking of taking Natalie there, I hope!"

Ryan shook his head. "Don't worry, we're not thinking of going in."

He is mother picked up her cup of tea. "Talking about Aunty Debbie, I'd like you to take a pair of bedroom curtains round to her for altering. She knows what to do."

"This evening?" Ryan asked quickly.

His mother laughed. "You sound very keen. You can take Natalie with you in the morning. I know

Aunty Debby wants to see Natalie. We could all go if we had the car."

"I'd like to go there on the bus, this evening," Ryan said, "as long as Natalie can come as well." He didn't intend to say much about their plans. Really, there was no need to say anything at all. But Natalie seemed to have different ideas. She went across to her mother.

"Mom, we'd specially like to go this evening because there's going to be a sort of adventure."

"Adventure? What sort of adventure?"

Then the story came out. The bikers in the park, the mention of the Seventeen Steps, and the "job" they were doing at seven.

Neither Ryan's nor Natalie's mother seemed to believe them.

"You've both got good imaginations," Natalie's mother said, laughing. She had an American accent exactly like her daughter. "Those bikers might be anywhere this evening. Besides, they more than likely saw you both hiding, and said it for fun. That's what I'd have done if I'd seen two nosey kids hiding in the bushes."

"We weren't hiding so we could listen," Ryan protested, finding his Aunty Lauren ever so easy to get on with. "We were hiding *from* them."

"So can we *please* go?" Natalie begged. "Please, Mom, say we can go today."

Both mothers looked at each other and smiled.

Ryan's mother laughed. "Oh to be young again! All right, but take the parcel of curtains to Aunty Debbie first. I don't want them getting lost in the fun and games!"

Natalie's mother looked serious for a moment. "Stay together, and make sure you both have your phones in case you get separated. And if — and I mean *if* — you see anything suspicious happening, keep well clear and phone for the police. Don't try to be heroes."

Ryan was pleased, of course, that they were allowed to go. He was also pleased that Natalie had spoken up and said what they were really going to do. Natalie was like that. She spoke up and seemed to tell the truth. Ryan felt ashamed when he thought of the way he sometimes deceived his parents.

Aunty Debbie often did work for the family on her sewing machine. She was younger than Ryan's mother — who was her sister — and hadn't been married long. She and her husband, Uncle Miles, lived in a flat at the top of a large house the other side of town. Ryan never saw very much of them and didn't think of them as fun to be with anyway, unlike his other uncles and aunts.

One thing he did like was Aunty Debbie's sewing machine. It was very modern and did all sorts of fancy stitches that fascinated him. He started to describe the machine to Natalie but was interrupted by his mother who came back into the room from using the phone.

"Aunty Debbie won't be in this evening, so you'll have to leave the parcel with the people in the flat below. They won't mind, I'm sure."

Ryan was almost afraid to ask the question that needed asking. "Can we really go to the Seventeen Steps after we've left the parcel?" It was best to check, in case there'd been a misunderstanding.

His mother laughed. "If I thought there was anything in this, I'd go along as well." She caught hold of Ryan's hand and turned him to face her. "Any adventure there is, will take place in that head of yours! Seventeen Steps indeed! And make sure you're back by eight."

"Yes, Mum, promise," Ryan said.

"I know your promises, my lad. What about Natalie?"

"Natalie will keep with me, Mum, all the time. Won't you, Nat?"

Natalie promised to stick with him. "Yes, Aunty Sarah and Mom, I really do promise. Honestly."

Ryan's mother, who was Aunty Sarah to Natalie, took one look at the two eager faces and smiled. "Not a minute after eight, Ryan," she warned, "or I'll never trust you out again."

Ryan and Natalie stayed around the house for the rest of the afternoon, just talking about things. Nothing was said about the Seventeen Steps during tea, and Ryan hoped that was how it would stay.

At six o'clock Ryan and Natalie were ready to leave.

"Right now, wrap up warm and be off," Ryan's mother said. "I'll get the parcel from upstairs. I've put the money for the bus on the kitchen table. And take care."

With the parcel in Ryan's hands, he and Natalie quickly left the house before their mothers changed their minds.

Some heavy clouds had come over, making the evening seem very gloomy. The buses ran every few minutes and the journey would take about a quarter of an hour. Ryan had been across the city on his own several times to see his Aunty Debbie — in daylight. As soon as they dropped off the parcel, he knew the way to walk to Walton Street. How exciting this was!

Chapter Eleven

Just as the bus was coming, Ryan realised he hadn't picked up the money for the bus fare from the kitchen table. He felt in the pocket of his jeans and found he had more than enough for the single journey, but not enough for getting home. There was no way he was going home now and risk missing the robbery. Natalie would have to pay on the way back.

The bus was almost empty when it came. Ryan paid the fare, and he and Natalie went upstairs, which he knew was always the best way to travel on a double-decker. The bus passed through the city centre where it began to fill up. The shops were brightly lit, and the advertising signs flashed on and off around the large square. The bus jerked on its way, carrying nearly a full load of passengers now.

Ryan glanced around and wondered what everyone was planning to do that evening. Most of the passengers would be on their way home from work or shopping. A few might be going out to visit friends. Probably no one was going to have an adventure. And even if they were, it would be nothing like the adventure he was sharing with Natalie.

Nobody seemed to take any notice of them sitting together. Ryan was glad. This adventure was just for him and Natalie — until the gang was caught. Then they could share it with everyone. They might even get on the television news!

As his mother had said, Aunty Debbie and Uncle Miles were out. Ryan had been hoping all the way that they would be. If he and Natalie had been asked in, they wouldn't have been to get away in time to go to the Seventeen Steps by seven, and be home by eight as promised.

As they walked together towards Walton Street, Ryan realised that Natalie's promises were different from his. Hers were meant to be kept. Perhaps knowing Jesus was your friend made it more important to keep a promise. Ryan shrugged. How could Jesus be your *friend*? All this was more than he could get his head round. Perhaps, as he'd said to Natalie earlier, perhaps things would get better as he got older. Not that Natalie had agreed with him.

Ryan looked at his watch again. They were going to be rather early. Still, it would be better that way. It would be silly to arrive late and find the Seventeen Steps had already been robbed!

Natalie spoke in a low voice. "I suppose we're going to the right place. You know, those bikers might be robbing somewhere with seventeen steps miles away."

Ryan felt sure they'd got it right. "Nothing else with that name around here came up on the internet. You wait, we'll find them there — at seven o'clock." It was an exciting thought.

Aunty Debbie's flat was several streets away from Walton Street and the Seventeen Steps. The pavements were full of people. Natalie said she was keeping close to him because she had no idea of the way. She didn't want to risk taking out her phone to check the map in the crowded streets. There were shops along each side of High Street, and just for a moment Natalie stopped to look at a display of shoes.

Ryan didn't notice. He carried on. Everyone seemed to be in a hurry. A large crowd was gathering outside a cinema. Ryan turned the corner and started down Walton Streets towards the Seventeen Steps. He turned to speak to Natalie but she wasn't with him.

"Nat!" he called, feeling certain his cousin was close by. Walton Street was quiet. Very quiet. And it was dark now. It was in the main road that there had been so many people. Perhaps Natalie was hiding in a doorway for fun. "Nat!" he called again. "Nat!"

An old man passed by. Ryan thought of the old whiskered squatter he'd encountered in the basement. He suddenly felt frightened. Frightened and alone.

He pulled his phone from his pocket and realized in alarm that he hadn't put Natalie's number in his phone book. He could only hope she had his. There was only one thing to do. He had to go back to the High Street. Natalie would be there. She was probably just as worried, looking up and down and wondering where he'd gone. Ryan could have kicked himself for going on ahead. He'd promised his mum he'd look after her. That had been a promise he'd meant to keep.

"Nat!" Ryan stood on the pavement in the main road. It was better to call out than just stand looking. Or was it? Several people were staring in his direction as though he was the local crazy. He walked back along the High Street, looking in shop doorways.

Natalie seemed to have disappeared. Then a sudden thought came to him. She was probably already at the Seventeen Steps waiting for him. She'd probably gone on ahead and now she would be waiting anxiously.

Ryan's phone rang in his pocket. It was Natalie asking where he was. He quickly explained which road to go down.

"I'll see you there in a couple of minutes," she said. "I thought I'd lost you for good. I knew I had your phone number written down somewhere. It was in my pocket, but I couldn't find it for ages."

He sighed with relief. Next time they went out,

he'd have Natalie's phone number saved on his mobile, and she would have his. They were *both* stupid — and he'd heard girls were more sensible than boys!

It wasn't far to the Seventeen Steps. They'd wasted a bit of time, but there were still ten minutes to go before seven o'clock.

Here was the place now, but no sign of Natalie. A billboard flashed on and off outside.

SEVENTEEN STEPS
LIVE MUSIC

It looked so mysterious and exciting — a tall building, with no lights in the upstairs windows. The entrance was down a long flight of brightly lit steps. *Seventeen Steps.*

"Look who it is!"

Ryan turned in surprise at the voice.

"It's that kid from the park!"

Ryan could see two bikers leaning against the wall. They were wearing torn jeans and black leather jackets covered in studs. They had body piercings and tattoos, and they seemed to know him. In that case he knew them. Yes, there were their two noisy motorbikes on the other side of the road. Placed for a quick getaway.

"Looking for someone, kid?" The biker with the dark hair had wandered across to Ryan. "Collecting more old junk?"

Ryan looked around. He felt really frightened now. If only Natalie would come and help. He was probably going to be kidnapped. They'd do that so he wouldn't be able to tell what they'd done. A robbery right in front of his eyes, and he was helpless.

"Ryan, what's going on?"

"Nat! Oh, Nat, come quick. It's a——"

The two bikers turned round, and one of them said, "Why, it's your partner in crime."

"You'd better watch out," Ryan shouted loudly. His voice seemed a little shaky.

The two bikers laughed. The taller one turned to his mate. "The others will be here soon. We might as well go on down. Hey, you two kids, keep an eye open for a van. When it comes, give us a shout."

"We're calling the police," Ryan told him. "We're not going to help you."

"Oh, Ryan, you shouldn't have said anything." Natalie sounded shocked that Ryan had given them away like that.

"I don't care," Ryan shouted. "I'm not going to help them rob this place." With that, he rushed at the taller biker. So suddenly did he rush that the biker was knocked to the ground, with Ryan landing on top.

Chapter Twelve

Ryan was as surprised as the biker as they both fell.

Natalie ran at the other one, but he was prepared for the attack and held her away.

The biker on the ground pushed Ryan off and jumped to his feet. "What's up, kid? You gone mad or something? I've got my best gear on."

Ryan looked at the biker's torn jeans and black leather jacket. That was his *best* gear? "You're robbers," he shouted. "And we're calling the police."

As Ryan stepped back, there was a screech of brakes. An old van stopped with a judder. Another youth and a girl jumped out. "Having trouble, Lofty?" the girl asked.

"This kid's mad," the taller biker said. He must be Lofty. "He thinks we're robbers!"

The girl laughed. "Sounds like a good name. The Robbers in Concert. Hey, how about it?"

The youth who'd arrived in the van shook his head. "No, we'll stick to the Seventeen Steppers now we've got a chance of a contract here. The more I think of it, the more I like it."

"But you *are* robbers, so you might as well call yourself robbers," Ryan protested.

The girl looked at the three youths. "You're right," she said. "The kid *is* mad."

"Well, if you're not robbers, what are you doing here?" Ryan demanded.

Lofty, who seemed to be in charge, stood well away. "Just stay where you are, kid, and I'll tell you. And no rushing at me. Okay?"

"You'd better be quick," Ryan told him. "Natalie's got her phone ready. We're going to call the police."

"We're here to get some money," Lofty said. "Only if you don't let us get down there you'll spoil everything."

"There you are," Ryan told him. "You're robbers, like I said."

Lofty shook his head. "Don't keep saying that. We're a pop group."

The other two youths and the girl laughed, "Well, a sort of pop group, only we're new, see. This is our first proper booking. It's just a start. Soon we'll be in the big money." He laughed at the others, and they seemed to share a private joke.

"You're not here to rob the place?" Ryan asked in astonishment.

"Rob them? Rob them when they've been decent enough to give us a trial? You've got to be joking."

The third youth laughed. "The customers who've paid to go may think *they've* been robbed.

Get it?"

Natalie said quietly, "I think we've made a mistake."

Ryan nodded in agreement. "We came here to stop you robbing the place. We heard you in the park saying that you were going to do a job here, and we thought...."

The youths and the girl burst out laughing.

"I feel silly now," Ryan muttered to Natalie. "I wish we hadn't come."

"I'm glad," Natalie said. "This is the best adventure I've ever had. Anyway, what would we have done if it *had* been a robbery?"

"I dunno," Ryan agreed. "I suppose it *has* been an adventure. Yes, of course, it has. *My* best adventure, too."

"Have you come all this way because of us?" the girl asked.

Natalie and Ryan nodded.

"Then you'd better hurry back. You'll be in trouble at home if you're out too late."

Ryan said, "We're not *that* young! Anyway, I don't think I've got enough for the bus. Have you got any money, Nat?"

"Nothing at all. Sorry, Ryan."

"Nat, you're *always* got money with you," Ryan said in alarm.

One of the youths laughed. "That's good. Fancy getting your girlfriend to pay when you take her out for the evening!"

The others joined in the laughter, and they sounded quite ordinary. So different than they'd seemed in the park.

"I didn't want to risk bringing my wallet in case there was trouble," Natalie admitted. "I'm sorry, really I am."

"Where do you live?" Lofty asked.

"By the park where we first saw you," Ryan said. "We'll have to walk, but we'll be ever so late back."

"You can't walk back alone in the dark," the girl told them. "Here, I've got some cash. Come on, kids, this is for your bus."

Ryan hesitated. Should he accept?

"Jump in the van. Sid will take you back."

Ryan turned to Natalie and then to the youth who'd made the offer. The idea was tempting, but he'd been warned many times never to take lifts from strangers. True, these youths probably meant no harm, and they were hardly strangers now. The Seventeen Steppers! That had been a surprise.

Ryan looked at Natalie and then at the girl in the blue jeans. "We'll go on the bus, if you can spare the money," he said. "We'll let you have it back next time we see you."

"Jump into the van," pressed the youth. "Go on, you'll be safe."

"I'd like to," Ryan said, "but we don't know you."

"That's right," the girl agreed. "Sensible kids. One day we won't be strangers. We'll be famous. Everyone will have heard of us!"

Lofty pointed down the steps. "If we don't get down there with our equipment we'll never be famous. This is the only place that wants us to play for them. We changed our name specially for them. So long, kids. See you around some time."

Natalie and Ryan took the money and waved goodbye. Then they hurried for the bus. This time Natalie kept very close to Ryan!

"They weren't so bad after all," Ryan said, while they waited at the bus stop. "They didn't say sorry for what they did to the old Bible and the camera, though."

Natalie laughed. "You didn't say sorry for pushing Lofty to the ground. Besides," she sounded very forgiving, "it was decent of them to let us have the money for the bus. But," she added after a long pause, "I can't say I like them very much, all the same."

Ryan said, "I hate them. And we've got to see them again. You promised to give them back the bus money. They mightn't be so friendly next time we meet!"

Chapter Thirteen

"We've got a surprise for you, Gran!" Ryan couldn't keep the excitement out of his voice.

"A surprise, dear? For me? How nice."

Natalie and Ryan stood in Gran's kitchen. They'd gone round first thing the next morning.

"Open it, Gran," Natalie said. "You'll *never* guess what it is."

She examined the wrapping. "A book?"

"Do as Natalie says, Gran, and open it."

Gran untied the large bow of ribbon. Natalie had done the parcel up neatly in gift-wrap covered with pictures of red roses. "Photos? But who of? It's not you two. It's ... look ... my two boys! Your fathers! Now where did you two get hold of these pictures?"

"Do you like them, Gran?" Natalie asked.

"I most certainly do, dear. They're one of the nicest presents I've ever been given. But do tell me where you found them."

Ryan and Natalie explained about the old film that had been in the camera. They explained how they'd asked the photographer to make the prints and put them in the frame.

"We didn't know for absolutely sure they were our dads," Ryan admitted. "We couldn't ask anyone in the family without giving our secret away."

Before he knew what was happening, Ryan found himself being hugged. Instead of struggling to get away, he gave in. Then he hugged Gran in return.

"You're a kind boy, Ryan, a very kind boy."

"Natalie thought of it as well."

"I'm sure she did."

Natalie received a hug, too.

"You're both very kind to me. Now then, I seem to remember there were once two of my grandchildren who were keen to get an old Bible mended."

Natalie looked rather awkward. "We haven't forgotten, Gran. It's just that we've been having a bit of an adventure."

"An adventure? Ah, what fun it is to be young."

Fun? Ryan thought to himself. We've got to find the bikers again and give them their money back. *That* should be fun!

"Gran," he said suddenly, "what did you mean about treasure in the Bible?"

Gran smiled. She asked Ryan to bring the pages of the old family Bible across from the shelf by the window of her sitting room. They'd all been stacked together in the right order and would soon be put back inside the cover. Ryan fetched them and let them drop on the kitchen table with a thump.

"It's very difficult to find treasure without a light," Gran said quietly. Ryan and Natalie sat down by her side and listened. She seemed to know so much.

"Find the Gospel of John," she told Natalie, "and then find verse six of chapter one."

Natalie found the place in the old pages quite easily. There was a picture of rays of light shining out from the sun in the old engraving at the top of the page.

"This is a book written by the apostle called John, and verse six is about another John. John the Baptist. Read it and you'll see that John the Baptist came to tell people about a very great light."

"Jesus," said Ryan, who had read on a couple of verses. "That light was Jesus."

"*Is* Jesus," Gran corrected him. "He's the same light now as he was then. He wants to come into everyone's life and shine out brightly."

"Inside me?" Ryan asked. "I don't think I'd like that very much. The light would shine into all my dark corners."

"But it would brighten them up," Natalie told him.

Gran looked at Natalie. "You know what it means to have the light of Jesus inside, don't you, dear?"

Natalie nodded.

Ryan frowned. "But where's the treasure?"

Gran smiled, almost to herself. "The light is the treasure. The light is Jesus. There isn't anybody in the whole world who wouldn't be satisfied with that treasure, if only they could get it."

"So how *can* they get it?" Ryan asked, forgetting what Natalie had already told him.

"Not by trying, that's for sure. Just by asking."

"But suppose someone isn't good enough, Gran?" He remembered now what Natalie had said, but he needed to be sure.

"As it happens, no one is. No one at all. Never has been, never will be. Not me, not you, not anyone. That's why Jesus had to come and die and then rise from the dead."

Ryan suddenly understood. He remembered things he'd heard before. How God loved everyone in the world. Even the very worst people. He knew he wasn't one of the worst, but he often wondered how bad God thought he was. Natalie somehow seemed to have got it all worked out."

Gran went on to read from verse sixteen of chapter three, how God loved the world so much that he sent his Son, Jesus, to live here and then be punished on a cross. She explained that the punishment was instead of God punishing him — or Natalie — or anyone else for that matter.

Ryan bit his bottom lip. Did Jesus want to come inside him like a great bright light? A great bright light to drive out all the bad things and then show him the way through life?

"Will it work, Gran?" he found himself asking.

"Will what work, dear?"

"Will Jesus hear me if I ask him into my life, to shine inside like a great bright light?"

Natalie answered this time. "It worked with me, Ryan. One day I knelt down and said how sorry I was for all the things I'd ever done wrong. Then I asked Jesus to forgive me. I asked him into my life to share it with me. Yes, it worked with me."

"And with me," Gran said, and Ryan noticed tears in her eyes. "Only I wasn't so little when I asked him. I wish I'd done it when I was young like you."

"Why didn't you, Gran?" Ryan asked.

"I thought I could sort out my own life. Then one day I felt Jesus was ever so close and I just asked him into my life like Natalie did. Like thousands and millions of other people have done."

"Sometimes the light seems to get dim," Natalie said thoughtfully.

Gran smiled. "That's where this comes in." She tapped the Bible. "Reading it and talking with your heavenly Father every day. Think it over, Ryan. If you want that light in your life, the light of Jesus, then you have to ask him. It won't happen by itself."

"And you're sure he'll hear?" Ryan asked.

"Definitely," Natalie and Gran said together.

They smiled at each other, and Ryan realised they shared something he didn't — yet!

"And now," Gran said, "I've got a surprise for you, although it isn't as nice as the one you gave me."

She reached over to the table and picked up a small MP3 player with speakers.

"The pastor came looking for you. He said he's booked a Christian pop group at the hall for Friday week. He's doing what he calls advertising, and lending some of their recordings. He wants you to listen to them and play them to your friends. Then you can invite them along."

"That's good," Ryan said, "although Nat won't be able to go. She'll be back in America, but I have a couple of friends who might be interested. We'll play the music to you first."

Gran put her hands to her ears and pretended to be horrified. "Not again! The pastor played one of them for me, but I think I'm too old-fashioned for that sort of music. The old hymns are good enough for me, but if you young people find these things help you, I know God wants you to enjoy them."

Natalie and Ryan smiled at each other. They were very fond of Gran.

Gran added, "It's too fine to stay indoors. Why not take this box of noises into the park and listen to it? Only, get as far away from anyone else as you can. Music played in the park can be a nuisance, even if it's Christian music."

It sounded a good idea. Ryan peered at the MP3 player and read the title.

"That's strange," he said in surprise.

"What is it?" Natalie asked, as she put her head down to see.

THE LIGHT STEPPERS
STEPPING IN THE LIGHT
WITH JESUS

Ryan laughed. He thought of their adventure at the Seventeen Steps. "If I'd made this recording," he told Natalie, "I'd have put seventeen tracks on it and called it *Seventeen Steps with Jesus*. That *would* be funny. Then we'd get Lofty and his friends to record it, because they're the Seventeen Steppers." He rolled his eyes. "As if they would!"

"Perhaps God would like them to," Natalie said, sounding quite serious. "All sorts of strange things happen to people when you start praying for them. All sorts of strange things."

Ryan frowned. "Have you been praying for me, then?"

Natalie nodded. "A lot."

"Thanks," he said quietly. "I mean it. And have you been praying for that gang with the bikes?"

"A bit," Natalie admitted. "But it's not easy to

pray for someone you don't like. Not all prayer is easy anyway."

They had reached the park now, and they sat on the nearest bench. Ryan kept thinking how strange it was that not only their adventure, but this recording too was all about steps. He thought of the step he could take to ask Jesus to be his friend. If he took it, he would walk with the light of Jesus inside just like Natalie and Gran did. Perhaps after that he could pray for other people.

Natalie switched on the player. "Ready?"

But Ryan was staring into the distance. "Look, Nat, there's Lofty and his gang again."

Sure enough, there they were, the four who'd been at the Seventeen Steps. Two of them had acoustic guitars slung over their shoulders, but there was no sign of their bikes.

Natalie sprang up and went towards them.

"Hey, Nat, what are you doing? We don't want this player smashed up like the Bible. And think how they threw the camera around. It isn't ours anyway, it belongs to Gran's pastor."

"We owe them our bus fares. Don't worry, I've got some money!"

Natalie was running by this time, and Ryan had to follow with the player hidden behind his back. Lofty was the first to notice them.

"Those kids again," he called.

"That's right," Natalie said. "Those kids want to

pay you back their bus fares. Thanks very much. We got home safely."

Nobody spoke for a moment, and then Natalie asked, "Have you still got your booking?"

"Yeah! We were just smashing."

Smashing! Ryan thought of what they'd done to the old Bible. The word smashing described them perfectly, but he said nothing.

Then Lofty saw the player. "You kids have always got something. What's it this time?"

Ryan drew back, afraid of what was coming. But Natalie spoke out.

"Something in your line. Switch it on, Ryan."

Ryan pressed the switch. There was the sound of guitars and drums. Then the vocal with a chorus about Jesus.

Before Ryan could feel embarrassed, the others edged nearer. It was a catchy tune.

Lofty pointed at the player. "Let's have that track again."

Ryan did as he was told, while the two guitarists played the backing between them. As the chorus began again, they started to accompany the tune. The girl joined in the occasional word.

They ran the track twice more.

"Like to hear the next one?" Ryan asked.

All of a sudden the group looked foolish, as though they'd been caught doing something silly.

"No thanks," Lofty said. "We're not religious,

but that stuff isn't bad."

They moved off, but Ryan called after them.

"That group's coming to St. Mark's Hall on Friday of next week. You'd better come and hear them."

"You might be lucky," the girl called over her shoulder.

Natalie turned to Ryan. "See? All sorts of strange things happen when you pray!"

"But look at them," Ryan protested. "All those body piercings and tattoos. I can't think Jesus would want anyone like that. And they're nasty people anyway."

"You just don't get it, do you," Natalie said. "Jesus wants *everybody*, no matter how they look or what they've done. I can't think he'd be all that bothered about tattoos and body rings."

Chapter Fourteen

The next morning, Natalie remembered the film they'd left at the camera shop. "We'll go and collect it now," she said. "I think I've got enough money."

Ryan laughed. "I'll go halves with you. I've had some more pocket money now." He suspected that Natalie's money was running low. That wallet hadn't contained the great wealth he'd imagined!

There was the other treasure, though. The proper treasure he'd found alone in his room last night. He knew now what it meant to have Jesus as a light, as a friend, and as a Saviour who had forgiven him. God was his heavenly Father. And what a difference it was going to make to his life! He asked Natalie why she hadn't told him about it all earlier.

"I did," Natalie said. "Several times, but you didn't understand. Don't you remember?"

"You're right, Nat, you did. Now I'm going to tell *everyone.*"

"*Everyone?*"

Ryan smiled. "Well, lots and lots of people. I'm going to get a Bible of my own. A modern one. Gran says modern ones say the same things, but they're easier for some people to understand."

They'd reached the camera shop. Natalie paused outside. She said she was sure she would look absolutely terrible in all the pictures. The man had said he'd scan the negatives so they could see them on the monitor. She made Ryan promise not to look at them until she'd asked the photographer to delete the ones she didn't like.

To her surprise, and Ryan's, they were all good. They selected the best of Natalie, and the only one there was of Ryan, and ordered prints to fit a frame just like the one they'd bought earlier for Gran.

"Nat," Ryan said, when they were outside, "let's go to the park. It's a lovely day and all I want to do is to sit down and think."

So they sat on a bench beside some tall trees. It was a dull autumn day and soon it might rain. Ryan didn't notice. The sun shone *inside* for him!

"Nat, when we get Gran's old Bible put back in its cover, let's put some extra pages."

"For family names?"

"For family photos. Then in hundreds of years' time the people in our family will know what we all looked like."

Natalie nodded slowly. "That's the greatest idea ever. I wish all the others had done it. They're only names now. I wonder what some of them did look like? They might have looked like us."

"P'raps it's not too late," Ryan said, as he looked up at the leaves tumbling down slowly against the grey sky. "We'll ask around and see what old photographs there are in the family, and you can copy them on your phone."

"How about a selfie of the two of us?" Natalie said. "We're going back in a couple of days, and I want to remember this vacation, the best one ever. You can have a copy."

The selfie taken, Natalie stood up, but Ryan stayed put.

"Not yet, Nat. I just want to stay here and think."

Natalie's phone rang. "Yes, Mom. What, on my own?" She turned to Ryan. "Mom wants me to go back. There's something she wants to discuss with me in private."

"Discuss what?" Ryan asked.

Natalie shrugged. "No idea. It's private." She smiled. "I expect you'll find out soon enough. Don't be long."

Ryan watched her go. There was so much to think about. A few days ago he'd not even met Natalie. Now, here she was, all the way from America and sharing his adventures. The adventures with the Seventeen Steps had been *his* best ever, too. If he saw the bikers again he'd remind them of the pop concert at the church hall.

Perhaps he would be asked back to America soon. He could certainly hope so.

Gran's old folding camera was one of his most

precious possessions. Well, his and Natalie's. Then there was the treasure trail in the old family Bible that Gran had told him about. Jesus, the Light of the World, and now his Light too. As soon as he got his own Bible he'd read bits of it every day. Natalie had something she called Bible notes. She was going to show them to him that evening.

Natalie was the best cousin anyone could have. There must be something he could do for her. A surprise present. What had Natalie said about surprise presents? You gave them on a day when the person wasn't expecting a present. Then it really *was* a surprise. All right, but what?

He turned quickly at the sound of a motorbike. His heart sank as he recognised it. And he didn't even have Natalie with him!

"Hey, kid, where's your girlfriend?"

There was just one bike. The girl on the back held something large. "You're not such bad kids. We ... well I ... we, kind of felt sorry for messing you about. That old Bible...." She shook her head, clearly embarrassed.

Lofty sat on the front, his visor raised. "Only we didn't know where you lived."

Just as well, Ryan thought.

"So we've brought you a pressie to make up for it," the girl said. "It's an old Bible we bought in town." And she held it out.

Ryan felt cautious. It could be a trick.

"Well," Lofty said, "aren't you going to take it? It says on the front it's light, only it ain't. It's heavy!" And he laughed.

"Go on," the girl urged. "It will make up for what we did."

Slowly, Ryan stepped forward. "Thanks," he said. "Thanks."

He took it and stepped back.

Then he added, "Don't forget the music in the church hall on Friday next week."

Lofty revved the bike up. The girl on the back shouted out, "We'll see what we're dong that evening." And then they were gone.

An old family Bible. That's what Natalie would like. Never mind taking photographs of all the names in Gran's one. If they had time, he and Natalie could copy every name and date out into this one by hand, and Natalie could take it back to America with her.

Natalie said a present was only a surprise if you weren't expecting it. Well, this old Bible would certainly come as a surprise!

"Natalie," he said, gasping for breath when he got home with the heavy Bible under his arm, "you'll never guess what..."

Natalie held up her hand. "Calm down, calm down. I've got some *great* news."

"Yes, but you'll never guess what...."

"Let me go first. Dad came over for an interview

for a job here in England. That's what the secret was all about. And he's got it. He starts straight after Christmas!"

Ryan put the Bible down. His arm was aching. "Does that mean you and your mum will be coming over to live here?"

"Yes, of course. We'll be seeing ever such a lot of each other." She winked at him. "We might even have another adventure."

Ryan grinned. "Or maybe more than one. And look what I've brought back from the park. It's a surprise present — for you. From Lofty and his friends!"

THE END

Your word is a lamp to my feet
and a light to my path
(Psalm 119:105)

Jesus spoke to them, saying, "I am the light of the world. Whoever follows me will not walk in darkness, but will have the light of life" (John 8:12).

There was a man sent from God, whose name was John. He came as a witness, to bear witness about the light, that all might believe through him. He was not the light, but came to bear witness about the light.

The true light, which gives light to everyone, was coming into the world. He was in the world, and the world was made through him, yet the world did not know him. He came to his own, and his own people did not receive him. But to all who did receive him, who believed in his name, he gave the right to become children of God, who were born, not of blood nor of the will of the flesh nor of the will of man, but of God (John 1:1-13).

About White Tree Publishing

White Tree Publishing publishes mainstream evangelical Christian literature in paperback and eBook formats, for people of all ages, by many different authors. We aim to make our eBooks available free for all eBook devices, but some distributors will only list our eBooks free at their discretion, and may make a small charge for some titles — but they are still great value!

We rely on our readers to tell their families, friends and churches about our books. Social media is a great way of doing this. Please pass the word on to Christian TV and radio networks. Also, write a positive review on the seller's/distributor's website if you are able.

The full list of our published and forthcoming Christian books is on our website
www.whitetreepublishing.com.
Please visit there regularly for updates.

Chris Wright has three grownup children, and lives in the West Country of England where he is a home group leader with his local church. More books by Chris Wright for young readers are on the next pages. His personal website is:
www.rocky-island.com

More books by Chris Wright

The Two Jays Adventure
The First Two Jays Story
Chris Wright

James and Jessica, the Two Jays, are on holiday in the West Country in England where they set out to make some exciting discoveries. Have they found the true site of an ancient holy well? Is the water in it dangerous? Why does an angry man with a bicycle tell them to keep away from the deserted stone quarry?

A serious accident on the hillside has unexpected consequences, and an old document "all in foreign" may contain a secret that's connected to the two strange stone heads in the village church — if James and Jessica can solve the puzzle. An adventure awaits!

eBook ISBN: 978-0-9954549-8-9

Paperback ISBN: 978-1-5203448-8-1
5x8 inches 196 pages
Available from major internet stores
$5.99 £4.95

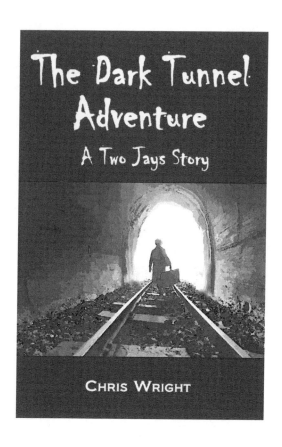

The Dark Tunnel Adventure
The Second Jays Story
Chris Wright

James and Jessica, the Two Jays, are on holiday in the Derbyshire Peak District, staying near Dakedale Manor, which has been completely destroyed in a fire. Did young Sam Stirling burn his family home down? Miss Parkin, the housekeeper, says he did, and she can prove it. Sam says he didn't, but can't prove it. But Sam has gone missing. James and Jessica believe the truth lies behind one of the old iron doors inside the disused railway tunnel.

eBook ISBN: 978-0-9957594-0-4

Paperback ISBN: 978-1-5206386-3-8
5x8 inches
Available from major internet stores
$5.99 £4.95

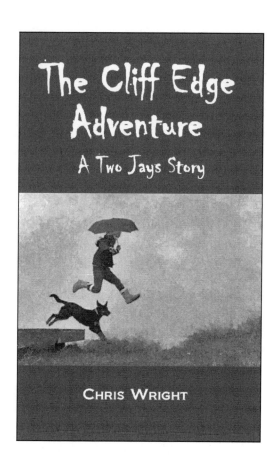

The Cliff Edge Adventure
The Third Two Jays Story
Chris Wright

James and Jessica's Aunt Judy lives in a lonely guest house perched on top of a crumbling cliff on the west coast of Wales. She is moving out with her dog for her own safety, because she has been warned that the waves from the next big storm could bring down a large part of the cliff — and her house with it. Cousins James and Jessica, the Two Jays, are helping her sort through her possessions, and they find an old papyrus page they think could be from an ancient copy of one of the Gospels. Two people are extremely interested in having it, but can either of them be trusted? James and Jessica are alone in the house. It's dark, the electricity is off, and the worst storm in living memory is already battering the coast. *Is there someone downstairs?*

eBook ISBN: 978-0-9957594-4-2

Paperback ISBN: 9781-5-211370-3-1
$5.99 £4.95

The Midnight Farm Adventure
The Fourth Two Jays Story
Chris Wright

What is hidden in the old spoil tip by the disused Midnight Mine? Two men have permission to dig there, but they don't want anyone watching -- especially not Jessica and James, the Two Jays. And where is Granfer Joe's old tin box, full of what he called his treasure? The Easter holiday at Midnight Farm in Cornwall isn't as peaceful as

James's parents planned. An early morning bike ride nearly ends in disaster, and with the so-called Hound of the Baskervilles running loose, things turn out to be decidedly dangerous. This is the fourth Two Jays adventure story. You can read them in any order, although each one goes forward slightly in time.

eBook ISBN: 978-1-9997899-1-6

Paperback ISBN: 978-1-5497148-3-2
200 pages 5x8 inches
$5.99 £4.95

The Merlin Adventure
Chris Wright
When Daniel, Emma, Charlie and Julia, the Four
Merlins, set out to sail their model boat on the old
canal, strange and dangerous things start to
happen. Then Daniel and Julia make a discovery
they want to share with the others.
eBook ISBN: 978-0-9954549-2-7

Paperback ISBN: 9785-203447-7-5
5x8 inches 180 pages
Available from major internet stores

The Hijack Adventure
Chris Wright

Anna's mother has opened a transport café, but why do the truck drivers avoid stopping there? An accident in the road outside brings Anna a new friend, Matthew. When they get trapped in a broken down truck with Matthew's dog, Chip, their adventure begins.

eBook ISBN: 978-0-9954549-6-5

Paperback ISBN: 978-1-5203448-0-5
5x8 inches 140 pages
Available from major internet stores

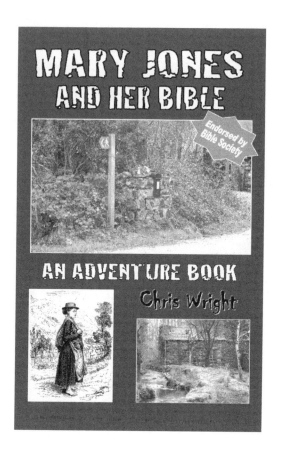

Mary Jones and Her Bible
An Adventure Book
Chris Wright
The true story of Mary Jones's and her Bible
with a clear Christian message and optional puzzles
(Some are easy, some tricky, and some amusing)

Mary Jones saved for six years to buy a Bible of her
own. In 1800, when she was 15, she thought she
had saved enough, so she walked barefoot for 26

miles (more than 40km) over a mountain pass and through deep valleys in Wales to get one. That's when she discovered there were none for sale!

You can travel with Mary Jones today in this book by following clues, or just reading the story. Either way, you will get to Bala where Mary went, and if you're really quick you may be able to discover a Bible just like Mary's in the market!

The true story of Mary Jones has captured the imagination for more than 200 years. For this book, Chris Wright has looked into the old records and discovered even more of the story, which is now in this unforgettable account of Mary Jones and her Bible. Solving puzzles is part of the fun, but the whole story is in here to read and enjoy whether you try the puzzles or not. Just turn the page, and the adventure continues. It's time to get on the trail of Mary Jones!

eBook ISBN: ISBN: 978-0-9933941-5-7

Paperback ISBN 978-0-9525956-2-5
5.5 x 8.5 inches
156 pages of story, photographs, line drawings and puzzles

**Pilgrim's Progress
An Adventure Book
Chris Wright**

Travel with young Christian as he sets out on a difficult and perilous journey to find the King. Solve the puzzles and riddles along the way, and help Christian reach the Celestial City. Then travel with his friend Christiana. She has four young brothers who can sometimes be a bit of a problem.

Be warned, you will meet giants and lions — and even dragons! There are people who don't want Christian and Christiana to reach the city of the King and his Son. But not everyone is an enemy. There are plenty of friendly people. It's just a matter of finding them.

Are you prepared to help? Are you sure? The journey can be very dangerous! As with our book *Mary Jones and Her Bible*, you can enjoy the story even if you don't want to try the puzzles.

This is a simplified and abridged version of *Pilgrim's Progress — Special Edition*, containing illustrations and a mix of puzzles. The suggested reading age is up to perhaps ten. Older readers will find the same story told in much greater detail in *Pilgrim's Progress — Special Edition* on the next page.

eBook ISBN 13: 978-0-9933941-6-4

Paperback ISBN: 978-0-9525956-6-3
5.5 x 8.5 inches 174 pages £6.95
Available from major internet stores

Pilgrim's Progress
Special Edition
Chris Wright

This book for all ages is a great choice for young readers, as well as for families, Sunday school teachers, and anyone who wants to read John Bunyan's *Pilgrim's Progress* in a clear form.

All the old favourites are here: Christian, Christiana, the Wicket Gate, Interpreter, Hill Difficulty with the lions, the four sisters at the

House Beautiful, Vanity Fair, Giant Despair, Faithful and Talkative — and, of course, Greatheart. The list is almost endless.

The first part of the story is told by Christian himself, as he leaves the City of Destruction to reach the Celestial City, and becomes trapped in the Slough of Despond near the Wicket Gate. On his journey he will encounter lions, giants, and a creature called the Destroyer.

Christiana follows along later, and tells her own story in the second part. Not only does Christiana have to cope with her four young brothers, she worries about whether her clothes are good enough for meeting the King. Will she find the dangers in Vanity Fair that Christian found? Will she be caught by Giant Despair and imprisoned in Doubting Castle? What about the dragon with seven heads?

It's a dangerous journey, but Christian and Christiana both know that the King's Son is with them, helping them through the most difficult parts until they reach the Land of Beulah, and see the Celestial City on the other side of the Dark River. This is a story you will remember for ever, and it's about a journey you can make for yourself.

eBook ISBN: 978-0-9932760-8-8

Paperback ISBN: 978-0-9525956-7-0
5.5 x 8.5 inches 278 pages
Available from major internet stores

**Agathos, The Rocky Island,
And Other Stories
Chris Wright**

Once upon a time there were two favourite books for Sunday reading: *Parables from Nature* and *Agathos and The Rocky Island.*

These books contained short stories, usually with a hidden meaning. In this illustrated book is a selection of the very best of these stories, carefully retold to preserve the feel of the originals, coupled with ease of reading and understanding for today's readers.

Discover the king who sent his servants to trade in a foreign city. The butterfly who thought her eggs would hatch into baby butterflies, and the two boys who decided to explore the forbidden land beyond the castle boundary. The spider that kept being blown in the wind, the soldier who had to fight a dragon, the four children who had to find their way through a dark and dangerous forest. These are just six of the nine stories in this collection. Oh, and there's also one about a rocky island!

This is a book for a young person to read alone, a family or parent to read aloud, Sunday school teachers to read to the class, and even for grownups who want to dip into the fascinating stories of the past all by themselves. Can you discover the hidden meanings? You don't have to wait until Sunday before starting!

eBook ISBN: 978-0-9927642-7-2

Paperback ISBN: 978-0-9525956-8-7
5.5 x 8.5 inches 148 pages £5.95
Available from major internet stores

Zephan and the Vision
Chris Wright

An exciting story about the adventures of two angels who seem to know almost nothing — until they have a vision!

Two ordinary angels are caring for the distant Planet Eltor, and they are about to get a big shock — they are due to take a trip to Planet Earth! This is Zephan's story of the vision he is given before being allowed to travel with Talora, his companion angel, to help two young people fight against the enemy.

Arriving on Earth, they discover that everyone lives in a small castle. Some castles are strong and built in good positions, while others appear weak and open to attack. But it seems that the best-looking castles are not always the most secure.

Meet Castle Nadia and Castle Max, the two castles that Zephan and Talora have to defend. And meet the nasty creatures who have built shelters for themselves around the back of these castles. And worst of all, meet the shadow angels who live in a cave on Shadow Hill. This is a story about the forces of good and the forces of evil. Who will win the battle for Castle Nadia?

The events in this story are based very loosely on John Bunyan's allegory *The Holy War*.

E-book ISBN: 978-0-9932760-6-4

Paperback ISBN: 978-0-9525956-9-4
5.5 x 8.5 inches 216 pages
Available from major internet stores

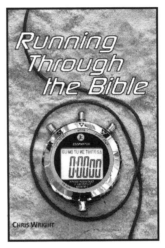

Two of four short books of help in the Christian life by Chris Wright:

Starting Out — help for new Christians of all ages. Paperback ISBN 978-1-4839-622-0-7, eBook ISBN: 978-0-9933941-0-2

Running Through the Bible — a simple understanding of what's in the Bible — Paperback ISBN: 978-0-9927642-6-5, eBook ISBN: 978-0-9933941-3-3

So, What Is a Christian? An introduction to a personal faith. Paperback ISBN: 978-0-9927642-2-7, eBook ISBN: 978-0-9933941-2-6

Help! — Explores some problems we can encounter with our faith. Paperback ISBN 978-0-9927642-2-7, eBook ISBN: 978-0-9933941-1-9

Printed in Great Britain
by Amazon